A Doll's Life

Book and Lyrics by
Betty Comden and Adolph Green

Music by
Larry Grossman

SAMUEL FRENCH

ISBN 978-0-573-69544-5

www.concordtheatricals.com
www.concordtheatricals.co.uk

MUSIC AND THIRD-PARTY MATERIALS USE NOTE

IMPORTANT BILLING AND CREDIT REQUIREMENTS

CHARACTERS

NORA HELMER (Nansen)
TORVALD HELMER
TRAIN CONDUCTOR
OTTO BERNICK, *musician*
HAMSUN, *owner of a restaurant*
JOHAN BLECKER, *lawyer*
ERIC DIDRICKSON, *business giant*
DR. BERG, *well to do doctor*
GUSTAFSON, *successful businessman*
PETERSON, *opera conductor*
ASTRID KLEMNACHT, *an opera diva*
MULLER, *the Cannery Foreman*
SELMA, *cannery worker, later Nora's personal maid*
JAILER
JACQUELINE LE BEAU, *a young Frenchwoman*
HUGO ZETTERLING, *coal industrialist*
KLOSTER, *lumber baron*
THE AMBASSADOR, LARS GRUNBORG,
    Norway's Ambassador to England
CAMILLA FORRESTER, *a beautiful actress*

Ladies of the Evening, Pimp, Female opera singers, Male opera singers, Call Boy, Karl the Stg. Mgr., Female guests at Audition, Male guest at Audition, Cannery Workers, Jailed Woman, Maids at Eric's Reception, Cafe Patrons, Cafe Waiter

Everyone except Nora, Otto, Johan, Eric, Torvald and Astrid will double or triple and play many roles.

TIME & PLACE

Norway in the late 19th Century
(1879 to 1885)

MUSICAL NUMBERS

ACT I

Scene 1:

A Woman Alone . . . . NORA, CONDUCTOR
Letter to the Children . . . . NORA
A Woman Alone . . . . NORA, CONDUCTOR, OTTO

Scene 2:

Arrival in Christiania . . . . NORA, CROWD

Scene 3:

New Year's Eve . JOHAN, ERIC, DR. BERG, GUFTAFSON

Scene 5:

Stay With Me Nora . . . . OTTO, NORA

Scene 7:

The Arrival . . . . ASTRID, GUESTS
Loki & Baldur . . . . OTTO, MALE & FEMALE SINGER
You Interest Me . . . . JOHAN
The Departure . . . . ASTRID, GUESTS

Scene 8:

Letter From Klemnacht . . . . ASTRID

Scene 10:

Learn To Be Lonely . . . . NORA

Scene 11:

Rats & Mice & Fish . . . NORA, SELMA, CANNERY GIRLS

Scene 12:

Jailer, Jailer . . . . FEMALE PRISONERS
Dearest Children . . . . NORA

Scene 13:

Loki & Baldur (off) . . . . ASTRID

MUSICAL NUMBERS

ACT II

Scene 1:

    You Puzzle Me .... JOHAN

Scene 2:

    No More Mornings .... NORA

Scene 3:

    Good Evening, Old Friend .... ERIC, MALE GUESTS
    There She Is .... JOHAN, ERIC, OTTO
    Power .... NORA

Scene 5:

    (Reprise) Letter To The Children .... NORA
    At Last .... JOHAN

Scene 6:

    Power .... CAFE PATRONS
    There He Is .... NORA, JACQUELINE
    Can't You Hear
        I'm Making Love To You? .... JOHAN, NORA

Scene 7:

    Finale .... NORA

ACT I

Scene One
NORWAY

(The train station. People rushing. Train noises. NORA making her way through the crowds on the platform.)

CONDUCTOR: *(On the platform)* Train for Christiania leaving on track four. Train for Christiania leaving on track four. All aboard! Grunstad! Next station, Grunstad! *(NORA enters the train – finds a seat in an empty compartment. Sounds of the train departing, turning into train pulse under – segueing right into "A Woman Alone". CONDUCTOR enters)* Tickets ... tickets please ...

(Music Cue 1A: A Woman Alone – Part I)

CONDUCTOR:	**NORA:**
WELL, WELL, WELL	
WHAT HAVE WE HERE?	
A WOMAN ALONE	A WOMAN ALONE
ON A TRAIN AT NIGHT ...	ON A TRAIN AT NIGHT ...
SHE MUST BE *THAT* KIND	HE THINKS I'M *THAT* KIND
OF WOMAN ... TO BE SURE	OF WOMAN I AM SURE
SHE HAS A STORY	WHAT KIND OF STORY
WAS SHE RUN OUT OF TOWN	CAN I INVENT
AND WARNED SHE'D	SO HE'LL ALLOW ME
BETTER STAY AWAY?	TO STAY

(Train pulse continues under.)

CONDUCTOR: Ticket, Miss? ... Madam ...
NORA: *(Very offhand)* Oh yes.

(She opens her bag casually.)

CONDUCTOR: Destination?

(Train pulse fades out.)

NORA: *(Cool, matter of fact)* Christiania. Our aunt ... taken seriously ill. My husband has been detained on business ... in Copenhagen. *(Rummaging in her bag)* Where *is* that ticket? I had no choice but to travel alone. Oh dear, I can't find it! Oh! My money purse ... it's gone!
CONDUCTOR: *(Skeptically)* Hmmm!
NORA: Oh, dear, oh dear ... I know I had it when I left. My husband bought the ticket, bid me good-bye and ...
CONDUCTOR: In Copenhagen?
NORA: It must have been stolen! I opened my bag to put the ticket in for safekeeping, and this dreadful man bumped into me.
CONDUCTOR: *(Giving her a knowing look)* Next stop is Grunstad! Out!
NORA: But I assure you ... *(Wide eyed)* Don't you believe me? *(Piteously)* Oh my poor aunt! Couldn't you let me stay on till Christiania? After all, who will know? *(Scrunching herself up in a corner, cutely small)* and how much space do I occupy, really? See how tiny I can be?
CONDUCTOR: *(Sizing things up)* Of course, Madam ... make yourself comfortable. Train's almost empty. After Grunstad I can transfer you to a private compartment.
NORA: Oh?
CONDUCTOR: Christiania. Six hours away.

(CONDUCTOR exits.)
(Music comes up, segues to music for "Letter to the Children".)

(Music Cue 1B: Letter to the Children – Part I)

NORA: *(Alone)*
WHY AM I HERE?
I KNEW WHEN I LEFT.
WHEN I LEFT I WAS CLEAR ...
NOW I'M HAVING TROUBLE HOLDING ON TO IT
I *MUST* HOLD ON TO IT
I MUST BE CLEAR ...
I MUST WRITE MY CHILDREN WHY I AM HERE ...

(Suddenly, in another area of the stage, the lights come up on TORVALD. He faces front as if speaking to her in another room. This is all in NORA's memory. The middle of an argument – TORVALD lividly screaming at NORA.)

TORVALD: Do you realize what you've done? Do you realize? You're not fit to bring up the children. *(NORA rises from her seat on the train and walks forward with her bag, facing front, in memory. The entire memory scene is played front. Neither NORA nor TORVALD looking at each other at any time during the scene)* What's this?

NORA: *(Shaken and shaking)* Sit down, Torvald. We must talk. *(TORVALD, stunned, does not sit)* We've never exchanged a word on any serious subject. You've called me your little skylark, your little featherbrain. I've been your doll wife, just as I was my father's doll child, and the children have been my dolls ... and that is what our marriage has been. And you're right. I'm not fit to bring up the children. I must educate myself ... and that's why I'm going to leave you.

TORVALD: Leave your home? Neglect your most sacred duties? To your husband and children?

NORA: I have a duty just as sacred ... to myself. I believe that before everything else I am a reasonable human being just as much as you are. Good-bye, Torvald.

(We hear a door slam. The sound reverberates.)
(She turns and again sits in her seat on the train.)
(Lights out on TORVALD. Lights restore on NORA on the train, back in the present.)

*(Music comes up and segues to music for the chorus of "Letter to
    the Children".)*
(She gets out writing paper and pencil as if to write.)

(Music Cue 1C: Letter to the Children – Part II)

NORA:
DEAREST CHILDREN, DEAREST DARLINGS
HOW TO TELL YOU. WHAT TO TELL YOU?
MAMA'S BEEN TOLD THAT SHE'S BAD,
AND A MAMA WHO'S BAD IS BAD FOR HER CHILDREN
NOW I DON'T THINK I'M BAD,
AND I KNOW I'M NOT A FOOL,
BUT THERE'S SO MUCH I DON'T KNOW ABOUT IN THE
    WORLD,
THAT I FELT I MUST FLING MYSELF OUT IN THE
    WORLD ...
MAMA'S GOING TO SCHOOL.

MAMA'S QUITE SURE THAT SHE'S GOOD,
BUT SHE HAS TO BE SURE SHE'LL BE GOOD FOR YOU
    CHILDREN
SO IN THE BOOK OF LIFE
I WILL QUESTION EVERY RULE ...
THEN I'LL COME BACK AND TEACH YOU ABOUT THE
    WIDE WORLD,
AND MY WISDOM WILL LEAD YOU THROUGHOUT THE
    WIDE WORLD,
LIKE A PURE BRIGHT THREAD FROM A SHINING
    SPOOL ...
MAMA'S GOING TO SCHOOL.

SO SAY YOUR PRAYERS
AND WASH YOUR HANDS,
AND SAVE ME EVERY TOOTH ...
AND I'LL BRING YOU A DOLL ... AND A DRUM ...
AND THE TRUTH!

MAMA LOVES YOU, MAMA LOVES YOU.
AND SHE'LL WRITE YOU EVERY DAY.

MAMA LOVES YOU, MAMA LOVES YOU
BUT SHE HAD TO GO AWAY ... TO SCHOOL.

(Train pulse starts again. A young man, OTTO BERNICK, shabbily dressed in cap and muffler, carrying a violin case, opens the door of the compartment and comes in. He sees NORA. He looks surprised.)

(Music Cue 1D: A Woman Alone – Part II)

OTTO: *(To himself)*
WELL, WELL, WELL, WHAT HAVE WE HERE?
A WOMAN ALONE

NORA:
A WOMAN ALONE

OTTO:
ON A TRAIN AT NIGHT

NORA:
ON A TRAIN AT NIGHT
WITH NO TICKET AND NO MONEY

OTTO:
SHE MUST BE THAT KIND OF WOMAN, DO I DARE?

(He sits back on the seat opposite her, pulls his cap over his eyes and tries to sleep.)

NORA:
WHAT KIND OF STORY CAN I INVENT
SO THAT HE'LL LEND ME THE FARE?
(Clears her throat, flirtatiously; to OTTO) (Spoken)
Good evening ... Do you play the violin?

OTTO: Madam, what could possibly have given you that impression?

NORA: Sir ... I see you have a delightful sense of humor ...

OTTO: Madam, I am trying to sleep.

NORA: A musician's life must be so fascinating.

(To herself – her conscience speaking out loud.)

(Music Cue 1E: A Woman Alone – Part III)

NORA:
(GAMES ...
YOU'RE PLAYING GAMES
YOU LITTLE FLIRT
YOU LEARNED TO FLIRT WHEN YOU WERE FIVE
DON'T CALL ME NAMES
I'M ONLY TRYING TO SURVIVE
CALL IT INVENTION.)

OTTO: I want to sleep.

NORA: I was just trying to make pleasant conversation to pass the time.

OTTO: You're not just trying to make pleasant conversation to pass the time. I'm not interested.

NORA: I see. A man alone on a train in the middle of the night although he might be a criminal, an anarchist, or a lunatic is assumed to be a pillar of society. But a woman! *(Wound up)* My aunt ... in Christiania ... is sick in the King Oscar Hospital. I put my ticket in my bag for safekeeping ... but this man bumped into me and ... *(To herself – her conscience speaking out loud)*
(LIES! A PACK OF LIES
IT'S NO SURPRISE
YOU LEARNED TO LIE WHEN YOU WERE FIVE
DON'T CALL THEM LIES
I'M ONLY TRYING TO SURVIVE
CALL IT INVENTION ...)
(Rummaging in her bag)
Oh, this is dreadful! My whole money purse is gone.

OTTO: Don't ask me for money! *(NORA starts to cry)* And don't cry for God's sake!

NORA: *(Crying)* Suppose this happened to your sister?

OTTO: *(Exhausted)* Be quiet! Here ... ! Here's enough for the fare!

(He hands her three bills.)

NORA: *(With genuine relief)* Three Kroner. Thank you. You've really saved me. You're very gallant.

OTTO: No ... just sleepy.

(CONDUCTOR enters.)

CONDUCTOR: Tickets! Tickets, sir? *(OTTO hands it to CONDUCTOR) (With oily familiarity)* Your private compartment is ready, madam.

NORA: In the bottom of my reticule I found this.

(She hands him money.)

CONDUCTOR: *(Confused)* I ... I was only trying to make you comfortable ...

NORA: Go! Just go! *(She hands CONDUCTOR money. He takes sit and exits. OTTO, quite awake, looks at her appraisingly. She makes small talk. He is taking a sausage and bottle of wine from his rucksack)* I do wish I were going to Christiania for a different purpose ... It's such a beautiful city ... To think that what I'm going to see there is the hospital ...

(He crosses over and sits next to her. She is terrified but tries not to show it.)

OTTO: *(Moving in)* I know this lacks something in elegance ... but do share a bit of bread and sausage with me?

NORA: What a beautiful sausage ... it looks delicious! ...

OTTO: Lots of garlic ... I won't have any either. *(He tosses it away. He holds out uncorked wine bottle to her)* To the long night ahead of us ... Your lips will add an extra bouquet.

NORA: *(Plowing on)* Oh, no, no, thank you! Well ... Have you any kind of glass? I think I would like a sip of wine ... I feel quite faint. My illness has been getting worse and worse ...

OTTO: Your illness? You're ill?

(Drawing back apprehensively, across to the far corner of his own seat.)

NORA: *(Wistfully)* Yes ... I know I made up that story about my aunt ... I suppose I couldn't admit it to myself ... I couldn't face it ...

(OTTO hesitates ... looks at the wine bottle and at her.)

OTTO: There's not much left ... You finish it. *(He puts the near empty bottle on the floor at her feet)* I'm ... I'm sorry you're sick. Get some rest. I'll ... I'll be here ...

(OTTO pulls his hat over his eyes. NORA sits back, truly exhausted now.)
(Train pulse comes up under and segues into song. The CONDUCTOR comes by and stops in the doorway.)

(Music Cue 1F: A Woman Alone – Part IV)

CONDUCTOR:
A WOMAN ALONE ...

OTTO:
A WOMAN ALONE ...

NORA:
A WOMAN ALONE ...

CONDUCTOR:
ON A TRAIN AT NIGHT

OTTO:
ON A TRAIN AT NIGHT

NORA:
ON A TRAIN AT NIGHT

CONDUCTOR:
WHAT DOES SHE DO TO MAKE MONEY?

NORA:
(I LEARNED TO LIE WHEN I WAS FIVE.)

OTTO:
WHY DID I GIVE YOU THAT MONEY?

NORA:
(I LEARNED TO FLIRT WHEN I WAS FIVE)
WHAT CAN YOU DO WITHOUT MONEY?
(I'M ONLY TRYING TO SURVIVE ...)

(The CONDUCTOR goes. OTTO sleeps.) (Disgusted with herself)

WELL, LITTLE STARLING, LITTLE SONGBIRD ...
HOW DID YOU GET OUT OF THAT FIX?
SAME OLD BAG OF TRICKS.

IS THAT HOW ALL YOUR BATTLES WILL BE WON?
JUST AS BEFORE?
YOU SLAMMED A DOOR ...
NOW WHAT DOORS WILL YOU OPEN?

(Train stops with train sounds.)

CONDUCTOR: Christiania! Christiania! Last stop. Christiania!

(NORA looks out, gets up with her bag. She starts forward.)
(Lights change. Immediate music up. Morning in the city.)
(Train stops with train sounds.)
(Music continues under, segueing into the next scene.)

Scene Two

(Christiania. NORA gets off the train carrying her bag. She is scared but tries not to show it. A group of LADIES OF THE EVENING greet her.)

(Music Cue 2: Arrival in Christiania)

LADY 1:
LOOKIN' FOR A PLACE TO STAY, MISS?
ROOM AND BOARD FREE.

LADY 2:
WHERE THEY LET YOU SLEEP ALL DAY, MISS?
WORK AT NIGHT, YOU SEE.

BOTH:
IF YOU STAY ATTRACTIVE
YOU'LL STAY VERY ACTIVE
BUSY AS A HONEY BEE.
LOOKIN' FOR A PLACE TO STAY, MISS?
TRY MADAM HEDWIG'S.

NORA: *(Music remains under)* No. I don't think so ...

MAN:
LOOKIN' FOR A PLACE TO WORK, MISS?

BOTH LADIES:
FOOD AND RENT FREE.

MAN:
YOU'LL BE WORKIN' LIKE A TURK, MISS.

BOTH LADIES:
BUT IT'S FUN, YOU'LL SEE.

MAN:
BOUNTIFUL AND BOUNCY

FLUTTERY AND FLOUNCY
IN A PINCH YOU'LL DO FOR ME.
LEARNIN' EVERY TRICK AND QUIRK, MISS.

ALL:
AT MADAM HEDWIG'S.

NORA: I ... No!

ALL:
TRY MADAM HEDWIG'S ...
OR MADAM ISLE'S ...
OR MADAM BIBI'S ...
BUT MADAM HEDWIG'S IS THE BEST IN TOWN.

NORA: No! *(They all disappear) (People begin appearing.
She goes up to one man)*
SIR, I CAN COPY LETTERS
ANY WORK TODAY FOR ME?

MAN: *(To a woman)*
MA'AM I DO FANCY SEWING
ANYTHING TODAY FOR ME?

WOMAN:
NOTHING TODAY, NOTHING.

NORA:
I'M SO HUNGRY, IT'S GETTING WORSE.
I'M AS EMPTY AS MY PURSE.

ALL:
NOTHING TODAY, NOTHING.

NORA: *(To various people)*
KITCHEN WORK
LAUNDRY WORK
NURSING WORK
SCRUBBING WORK

ALL:
NOTHING

WOMEN:
MADAM HEDWIG'S?

ALL:
NOTHING

WOMEN:
MADAM HEDWIG'S?

ALL:
NOTHING

WOMEN:
MADAM HEDWIG'S?

ALL:
NOTHING, NOTHING, NOTHING TODAY
NOTHING, NOTHING, NOTHING FOR YOU
NOTHING.

(They all disappear. NORA is left alone.)

NORA: I'm so hungry. *(Looking around)* Maybe this restaurant will give me something to eat.
HAMSUN: *(A restaurant manager, ogling her)* Good evening, young lady.
NORA: Good evening, sir. I'm so hungry. Please! Could you give me something ... ?
HAMSUN: *(Looking her over)* Hm ... Well ... I can use extra help for New Year's!
NORA: Oh, thank you, sir!

(They exit.)
(Blackout. In black, music starts.)

Scene Three
A CAFE – NEW YEAR'S EVE

(Suddenly there is the sound of lively music and New Year's Revelers cross, as well as Waiters and Waitresses, busily at work.)

(Four well-dressed Gentlemen drinking aquavit. They are all quite tipsy, especially JOHAN, a lawyer, a civilized man in his late 30s.)

(Music Cue 3: New Year's Eve)

ALL:
TO THE SPOUSE, TO THE WIFE
TO THE BEST THINGS IN LIFE
THAT ARE WAITING AT HOME NEW YEAR'S EVE

ERIC:
TO THE FIGHTS THAT BEGIN
WITH "WELL, WHERE HAVE YOU BEEN"
THAT ARE LOOMING AT HOME NEW YEAR'S EVE

DR. BERG:
TO THE BREAKFAST EACH DAY
HAVING NOTHING TO SAY

ALL:
FROM TOMORROW TILL NEXT NEW YEAR'S EVE
(ALL except ERIC)
HERE'S TO HER ...

ERIC:
HERE'S TO ME
TWELVE MORE MONTHS OF ENNUI

DR. BERG:
HERE'S TO THE SEASON OPERA BOX

GUSTAFSON:
HERE'S TO THE BEDROOM DOOR SHE LOCKS

JOHAN:
HERE'S TO THE BILLS THAT NEVER CEASE

ERIC:
HERE'S TO THE GIRL I CALL MY NIECE

ALL:
HERE'S TO BYGONE DAYS AND SIMPLE JOYS
HERE'S TO ACTING ONCE AGAIN LIKE BOYS

ERIC:
TO OUR WIVES ...

ALL:
TO OUR LIVES

GUSTAFSON:
TO THE YOUTH WE CAN NEVER RETRIEVE

ALL:
TO NEW YEAR'S EVE.

JOHAN: *(Unsteadily)* Gentlemen, it's late. If you'll excuse me, I'd like to get home to Katrine.

ERIC DIDRICKSON: *(An Industrialist, arrogant, ruthless)* You're a hypocrite, Johan. There's nothing you'd like to do less.

JOHAN: It's just as painful for her as it is for me. A marriage made in Hades.

ERIC: Sit down! Don't try to make the rest of us feel guilty.

(JOHAN gets up to leave.)

GUSTAFSON: *(A Politician)* Let's have another round before we go.

(Lifting his glass.)

MEN:
TO HER RELATIVES – TO THE DIN
OF HER RAVENOUS KIN

ERIC:
WHO MAKE HELL OF MY HOME NEW YEAR'S EVE

JOHAN:
LET THEM FEAST, LET THEM STAY
IT'S A SMALL PRICE TO PAY –

BERG:
MATRIMONY'S A USEFUL THING

JOHAN:
WHEN A GENTLEMAN NEEDS A FLING

BERG:
THE OTHER LADIES I ADORE
UNDERSTAND THAT I AM SPOKEN FOR

ALL:
BEING SAFELY, SURELY WED
KEEPS US FREE TO JUMP FROM BED TO BED
TO THE RING – TO THE VOW
TO THE PROMISE WE USED TO BELIEVE.
TO NEW YEAR'S EVE!

(NORA enters with tray of drinks.)

JOHAN: *(Lifting his glass to NORA. BERG grabs tray. ERIC pours)* Ah! An angel of mercy. Join us.

(They are all quite drunk.)

NORA: But, Sir!
ALL: *(Lift glasses)* Happy New Year.

(BERG gives her a glass of aquavit.)

NORA: Oh, no ... I mustn't!
JOHAN: Come, it's a special occasion.
NORA: The manager will have me arrested.

(They sit her down.)

JOHAN: *(Pouring the drink)* I'll defend your case.
NORA: *(Taking it)* Thank you. Well, Happy New Year.

(She drinks.)
(A Waitress enters, sees NORA drinking and rushes off to tell HAMSUN.)

THE MEN: Happy New Year.
NORA: *(To JOHAN)* You're a barrister?
JOHAN: Yes.
NORA: *(Strengthened by the drink)* Sir – There's something I'm trying to find out. Uh – I have a friend – and she – signed her father's name to this bond –
GUSTAFSON: A forger –
NORA: The law says a woman can't borrow money on her own.
JOHAN: I know these medieval laws. I have to work around them all the time.
ERIC: *(Coldly)* Forgery's a crime. Your friend should get thirty years.
NORA: *(Shocked)* Even if it was to save her husband's life?
JOHAN: *(Interested)* She has no previous criminal record?
NORA: Only stealing from her own household expense money to buy macaroons.
GUSTAFSON: Women! Give them a lavish monthly allowance and they're always coming up short.
JOHAN: I'm glad I'm not your wife.
GUSTAFSON: I'm glad, too.

(They laugh.)

JOHAN: There are special circumstances here. If I were

representing her, I'd have the jury weeping to a man and the judge kneeling to kiss the hem of her gown.

   NORA: *(Lighting up happily)* Ah!

   JOHAN: *(Playfully)* Of course, they'd probably give her a token sentence – three or four years.

(NORA stops and gasps.)

   DR. BERG: You look a little pale. As your physician I recommend a second aquavit.

(He pours, she tosses it off. They laugh. The Waitress enters, followed by HAMSUN who sees her drinking and rushes to the table.)

   HAMSUN: Nora! Gentlemen, I apologize for this –

   DR. BERG: Hamsun, this young woman is my patient. I prescribed it.

   HAMSUN: *(Confused, apologetic)* Oh, of course, Dr. Berg.

(He withdraws.)

   NORA: *(Looks at them)* Thank you, gentlemen, for the education. And thank you for having drinks with a low scullery maid instead of with your wives!

(She delivers this with mock flirtatiousness, but real acidity. They laugh and start to leave.)

   ERIC: Johan!
   JOHAN: *(Looking at NORA)* In a minute, Eric.

   ERIC, DR. BERG, GUSTAFSON: *(Exiting)*
TO THE SPOUSE,
TO THE WIFE,
TO THE BEST THINGS IN LIFE ...

   JOHAN: You're must unusual for a "low scullery maid".

NORA: *(Uneasily)* Mr. Hamsun would not like this.

JOHAN: I hope we didn't jeopardize your job. Please ... get yourself something you like for the New Year. *(He hands her some money)* And should you need further legal advice, here's my card.

NORA: *(Looking at his card)* Thank you, Mr. Blecker. And for the legal advice so far, here is your fee. *(She hands him back the money)* Happy New Year.

(NORA crosses away to clear things off.)

ERIC: *(Offstage)* Blecker! Johan! Blecker!

(JOHAN, taken aback and impressed, weaves unsteadily to the exit. NORA and Waitress resume clearing the table. HAMSUN enters.)

HAMSUN: Nora!

NORA: Oh, Mr. Hamsun, I promise this will never happen again.

HAMSUN: Well, it's New Year's Eve ... I'll keep you on.

NORA: Oh, thank you.

(The Musicians are leaving. OTTO stops when he sees her.)

OTTO: You! The train!

NORA: Of all the restaurants to pick.

HAMSUN: Leave her alone. She has work to do, Bernick.

OTTO: And you're not ill.

NORA: No ... I lied.

OTTO: I don't blame you. I can be quite a devil.

HAMSUN: Good night, Bernick.

OTTO: And a Happy ...

HAMSUN: *(Impatiently)* Yes, yes, Happy New Year. Happy New Year! ...

OTTO: *(Still lingering ... leaning toward NORA)* And to you, too ... a Happy ...

HAMSUN: Get out! Bow-scratcher!

OTTO: *(Angrily, exiting)* Excuse me ...

(But OTTO lurks in the background till later.)

HAMSUN: I can pay you only a kroner a week ...

NORA: Thank you, I can manage.

HAMSUN: Except for the holidays, business has been terrible.

NORA: Forgive me ... of course its terrible. The way the place is run. Food comes to the tables ice cold. The kitchen's too dark ... The cafe too bright. Discourages romance ... I talk too much.

HAMSUN: Yes, but you're a good worker. You're new to the city. No local relatives?

NORA: No, sir, I'm alone.

HAMSUN: This is a hard city to be alone in.

NORA: *(Sincerely)* You've made it easier, Mr. Hamsun.

HAMSUN: *(Insinuatingly)* I could make it even easier. Shall we talk about it over a little New Year's supper?

NORA: *(Getting the idea)* I don't think so, Mr. Hamsun ... Have I lost the job?

HAMSUN: Yes, you have.

NORA: I need it.

HAMSUN: Here are a few kroner for you. Good luck. Good night.

(OTTO unseen, goes, then HAMSUN.)

NORA: *(Ruefully)*
HAPPY NEW YEAR'S EVE

(She takes off cap and apron and exits.)
(Cross-fade to outside.)

Scene Four

(Street. Outside the cafe. Late night. We wee New Year's Eve

Revelers crossing noisily. OTTO enters and starts playing his violin, waiting for NORA who comes on in hat and coat.)

(Music Cue 4: Street Sequence)

OTTO: *(Plays a little figure on violin)* Hello!

NORA: So that's what you've been waiting around for ... Here! Three Kroner! This is what I owe you. I've been dismissed ... Now leave me alone.

(She throws the kroner into his violin case which is lying on the ground.)

OTTO: Please *(Gives back the money)* ... I'm sorry.

NORA: *(Softening)* Thank you, Mr. ...

OTTO: Bernick ...

NORA: My name is ... Nansen ...

OTTO: I knew what the manager was leading up to. I was listening. But you know, he must have thought you were encouraging him.

NORA: *(Astonished)* Me? You heard me! I said terrible things about his restaurant.

OTTO: Talking about lights and romance ... it ... it gave him a certain impression.

NORA: *(Furious)* Who are you to pass judgment on anybody! You! You attacked me on the train! And a happy New Year to you, too!

(She walks away. He follows.)

OTTO: I'm sorry. *(He plays)* Please forgive me. *(NORA stops)*
I'D LIKE TO BE FRIENDS.
(Spoken) Maybe I can help you get work. I know you carry dishes magnificently.
WHAT ELSE CAN YOU DO?

NORA: *(Half sung, half spoken)*
I CAN SEW ... KNIT ... CROCHET ...

COPY LETTERS
I CAN MAKE CLOTHES

OTTO: There's a girl in my rooming house who works backstage at the opera. Maybe she can speak to the wardrobe people.

NORA: *(Taken aback – warmly)* That's very kind of you.

(She offers her hand. He shakes it. They start walking.)

OTTO:
SO WE'RE FRIENDS ...

NORA:
YES.

OTTO: My case! *(Going to pick up his violin case)* Miss Nansen, would you care to ... maybe we could share a toast for the holidays ... together ... I mean ... I have some aquavit hidden away.

NORA: I have some hidden away too. *(Shyly)* But, no ... I don't think I ...

OTTO: And I have some cheese ... some smoked reindeer.

NORA: And a key to your room you can swallow after you've locked the door.

OTTO: Oh no! It would all be quite proper. There's a parlor downstairs ...

NORA: Well, I ...

(OTTO plays and sings.)

OTTO: *(Playing with a flourish)*
PLEASE COME, MISS NANSEN
COME WITH ME, MISS NANSEN
THERE'S REINDEER, CHEESE
THREE KINDS OF HERRING, TOO ...

NORA: *(They finish outside his door)* Well ... All right!

(He dashes in ahead of her.)
(Lights cross-fade.)

Scene Five

*(OTTO runs ahead to his room. NORA looks off into the parlor,
sees something, and almost hysterically runs into OTTO's
room.)*

OTTO: *(Surprised)* Oh! I was just bringing this down to the
parlor. You shouldn't be in my room ... your reputation.

NORA: *(Visibly shaken)* Couldn't we stay here, Mr. Bernick?
There was a man and his wife down there ... and a little child ... It
was so ... noisy!

OTTO: Yes, if you wish! Her, Miss Nansen. Sit. *(He
indicates bed. She looks around. There is no place ... The chest
has things on it; only the bed is available ... she hesitates. He
clears off the clothes)* Please forgive the mess. I hadn't meant you
to see it. *(NORA sits on the chest)* You're upset. *(Getting bottle
and glasses)* Maybe a little aquavit. *(He pours for her and for
himself. Music of "New Year's Eve" played sweetly)* To you, Miss
Nansen.

NORA: Nora. And to you, Mr. Bernick.
OTTO: Otto.

(They toast.)

(Music Cue 5: New Year's Eve Reprise)

OTTO:
TO THE HERRING ...
(They sip.)

NORA:
TO THE CHEESE ...

OTTO:
TO THE REINDEER ...
(Sip.)

NORA:
TO THE DRINK
(Sip.)

OTTO:
TO MY ROOM .. I DECORATED IT MYSELF ...

(They toast.)

(Music Cue 5A: Torvald Enters)

(In another area, TORVALD enters – young, in a open-collared shirt, holding a champagne glass and a bottle.)

TORVALD: *(Exuberantly)* To our first New Year's Eve – married! And to our first child to come.

NORA: *(Staring out front, back in her past; delighted)* Torvald! Champagne! But we can't afford it!

TORVALD: *(Laughing)* I know. I poured our cheap wine into this bottle. *(NORA laughs)* I'm drunk just breathing the same air you breathe! You'll never want for anything, Nora. While you're here at home I'll be out in the wild forest hunting for food and furs to wrap our many children in.

NORA: *(Ecstatically)* Oh, Torvald – you are my life!

TORVALD: How I love you. To endless New Year's Eves together!

(TORVALD exits.)

NORA: *(Back in the present, to OTTO)* We can go downstairs, if you like ...

(Music Cue 5B: Stay With Me Nora – Part I)

OTTO: *(Hesitantly)*
STAY WITH ME, NORA
STAY HERE WITH ME, NORA ...
THERE'S SO MUCH TALKING WE CAN DO ...

WE'LL SHARE OUR FANCIES AND OUR FEARS
EXPOUND ON MUSIC AND LIFE.
I WON'T PRY INTO YOUR PAST ...
AND WE'LL LEAVE THE DOOR OPEN TOO.

(Music continues. She hesitates, then sits.)

NORA: *(Making a toast)* Well. Here's to your being the greatest virtuoso since Paganini!

OTTO: No ... I'm afraid Mr. Hamsun was accurate about one thing. I'm just a bow-scratcher.

NORA: *(Indicating music all around)* All this music ...

OTTO: *(With boyish enthusiasm)* I'm a composer!

(He grabs up and proudly holds out in front of her an enormous musical manuscript.)

NORA: *(Excited)* A composer!

OTTO: Unpublished ... an opera. A Norwegian epic to make Wagner shake in his slippers ... *Loki and Baldur ...*

NORA: I've known it since childhood!

OTTO: *(Bursting with it)* Ah ... but I took the old legend and gave it a hidden political ... uh ... sociological meaning. Loki, the God of evil ... is really Sweden, Baldur is the spirit of Norway and independence!

NORA: How thrilling ... how daring! You must finish your work so it can be heard by the world!

OTTO: *(Despairing)* Who has the time? Bring me a sponsor ... a Norwegian Prince Esterhazy. I don't understand money. I can never save anything.

NORA: *(Maternally, humorous)* How can you when you give it away to strange ladies on trains?

OTTO: *(Suddenly)* I just want you to know that was my first experience at seduction. I was lonely and angry and thinking of my fellow musicians. I have to listen to their bragging ... their flaming conquests ... I never have anything to say. So I thought ... here was my big chance. Pathetic ... It's such a burden being a man.

NORA: *(Surprised)* I never knew a man felt it was a burden being a man.

(In the other area TORVALD, older, bearded, authoritative, middle class figure appears.)

TORVALD: *(Patronizingly)* Nora – has my little featherbrain been out wasting money again? Is the little squirrel sulking?

NORA: *(Shamelessly coy)* Torvald, your little squirrel will scamper about and do all her tricks if you'll be nice and do as she asks.

TORVALD: Nora, guess what I have here ... Money.

NORA: *(Overly grateful)* Oh thank you, Torvald, thank you. This will keep me going for a long time!

TORVALD: Well, you must see that it does.

(He exits.)

OTTO: *(Continuing his speech)* So much expected of you – keeping up appearances – Nora *(Pause)* Come back.

NORA: I'm back. Please keep talking. *(Music starts)* People should talk to each other ... I mean, especially men and women should talk to each other ... like people.

OTTO: We're talking ... like people.

NORA: Yes, we are.

(Music Cue 5C: Stay With Me Nora – Part II)

OTTO:
STAY WITH ME, NORA
STAY HERE WITH ME, NORA
THERE'S SO MUCH TALKING STILL TO DO
WE'LL SHARE OUR FANCIES AND OUR FEARS
AS EQUAL PARTNERS IN LIFE
ALWAYS HAPPILY AWARE
WE'RE A MAN AND A WOMAN TOO.
I WANT TO BRUSH THOSE CLOUDS OF SADNESS FROM
    YOUR FACE

AND TEACH YOUR TROUBLED EYES TO SHINE
STAY WITH ME, NORA
I PROMISE YOU, NORA
YOU CAN STAY YOURSELF ...
IF YOU'LL ONLY STAY AND BE MINE ...

NORA: *(To herself)*
HE KNOWS WHAT I'M FEELING
I FEEL I COULD HELP HIM
HE'S YOUNG ... SENSITIVE ... AND UNSURE ...
HE'S A DIFFERENT KIND OF MAN ...
FROM THOSE I HAVE KNOWN ...

AN ARTIST ... LIVING FOR ART ALONE.
"EQUAL PARTNERS IN LIFE"

NORA:	**OTTO:**
	I WANT TO BRUSH THE CLOUDS OF SADNESS FROM YOUR FACE
HOW THOSE SIMPLE WORDS SHINE!	AND TEACH YOUR TROUBLED EYES TO SHINE
CAN THIS BE THE ANSWER?	STAY WITH ME, NORA
CAN THIS BE THE ANSWER?	I PROMISE YOU, NORA

OTTO:
YOU CAN STAY YOURSELF ...

NORA:
SHOULD I STAY?

OTTO:
IF YOU'LL ONLY STAY AND BE MINE ...

(NORA moves toward the door. She looks at OTTO. She closes the door ... and walks back toward him. They stand facing each other. Tentative embrace. Dim out.)

Scene Six

(Music Cue 6: Carmen Music)

(Backstage at the Opera.)
(ASTRID's dressing room and other areas ... Between the acts of Carmen. Act has ended. Sound of ovation.)
(Stagehands hammer and Opera Singers cross intermittently during the scene. Stagehands carry flats across frantically.)
(NORA is lugging a load of costumes – looking as if she has been working very hard.)
(ASTRID KLEMNACHT, the diva, handsome, temperamental moves into her dressing room.)
(Enters fuming. Grabbing the STG. MGR.)

ASTRID: Karl, tell that butcher Peterson to come to my dressing room immediately.
STG. MGR.: Very good, Madame Klemnacht.

(He runs.)

CALL BOY: *(Calling)* Fifteen minutes, Madame Klemnacht, fifteen minutes. Fifteen minutes to Act Four.
ASTRID: Ugh ... that Peterson conducts all of Carmen as if it were Siegfried's Funeral March. *(NORA goes to help her)* Where's Gretchen?
NORA: She went home sick. I'm helping out. I'm Nora. Madam Klemnacht, I think you are magnificent as Carmen. Such a strong woman.
ASTRID: A bitch my dear ... but true to herself to the end!
NORA: *(Helping her with her next costume)* – and when you dress up like a man ... like *Fidelio* where the audience can see your fine figure and limbs ...

(PETERSON enters.)

ASTRID: Thank you my dear.
PETERSON: *(Outside. He knocks)* Madame Klemnacht ... Peterson ... you sent for me.

ASTRID: Wait there till I'm ready.

NORA: What power you must feel for a woman ... to have a career and to be so totally on your own!

ASTRID: Well, not totally on my own. *(Looks at NORA)* Isn't there a man in your life?

NORA: Oh, yes, he's a composer ... Otto Bernick. I made him quit his job and for a few months I've been working here so that he can finish this great nationalist opera he's writing ... *Loki and Baldur.* The leading role, Baldur, the young god, is to be played by a woman ... a soprano ...

(She is obviously hoping against hope to interest ASTRID.)

ASTRID: *(Dryly)* I'm sure. And I'd be perfect for the leading role in this nationalistic opera?

NORA: *(Excited)* Oh, yes ... if you would only ...

ASTRID: *(Crisply, but not unkindly)* Out, my dear ... Just get the costumes together ... and go! I'll come to the opening night at the Paris Opera! *(Calling)* Peterson! *(CONDUCTOR enters carrying the score. NORA starts leaving carrying a costume) (NORA leaves dressing room area. To PETERSON)* Peterson! This is Bizet, not Bellini ... Less legato ... more fire!

PETERSON: *(Yelling furiously)* But I was conductor for Emma Calve in Brussels!

ASTRID: *Streetcar* conductor!

(Afraid she's hurt her throat, she sprays it. NORA has been flustered by ASTRID's remarks. She goes to a costume rack and hangs costumes. As she is working, JOHAN BLECKER enters, going toward ASTRID's dressing room. He sees her. He pauses.)

JOHAN: Don't I know you? Of course ... the cafe! *(ASTRID and CONDUCTOR continuing in pantomime)* New Year's Eve! The girl who was so interested in forged signatures ... Johan Blecker.

NORA: Oh yes. Excuse me, Mr. Blecker.

(She turns back to the costume rack.)

JOHAN: I stopped going to the cafe. You weren't there. And besides the food was always ice cold.

NORA: I told Mr. Hamsun that, *(Quietly)* I told him ... well ... too much and that's why I'm here. And now I'm afraid I'm going to lose this.

JOHAN: Did you try to tell Astrid how to sing? *(PETERSON comes storming out. And as he passes them, JOHAN calls in to her)* I'll be right in, Astrid. I have a message for you from Eric.

NORA: *(Moving to go)* Please ... I'm detaining you.

JOHAN: *(Feeling he should explain)* I'm only her legal advisor. Eric's her friend. Now what's this about losing your job?

ASTRID: *(To another Singer stopping by her room)* I can't talk to you now.

(She indicates her throat.)

NORA: I'm afraid I offended Madame Klemnacht. I was presumptuous ... I know I was.

JOHAN: *(Intrigued by her)* Tell me, I'm your legal advisor too.

NORA: I mentioned to her something about this young composer I know.

JOHAN: *(Interrupting NORA)* And he's written something that would be perfect for La Klemnacht and you want her to hear it and she got impatient and threw you out.

NORA: Yes, but this is so special! If she could only hear this ... an epic of Norway and Sweden – "Loki and Baldur,"

(There is a pause as JOHAN looks at NORA.)

JOHAN: You're very determined when it comes to something you care about, aren't you, my little forger?

NORA: *(Shocked)* Excuse me.

(She turns to go.)

JOHAN: *(He stops NORA)* I'd like to hear more about your friend's epic.

ASTRID: Come in, Johan.

(He touches the costume NORA is carrying.)

JOHAN: *(Calling to ASTRID)* In a moment. *(To NORA)* Now this would look good on you! Why don't you put it on after the opera and come out and dine with me?
NORA: *(Taken aback)* Oh, Mr. Blecker ...
JOHAN: What you're wearing will do perfectly well.

(He looks at her expectantly.)

NORA: But ... this friend who wrote the epic is ...
JOHAN: *(Understanding)* Is more than a friend ... ?
NORA: Yes.
CALL BOY: Places, Madame Klemnacht! Places!
ASTRID: Johan!
JOHAN: *(Calling to ASTRID)* I'll be right there.
NORA: Goodnight.
JOHAN: *(To NORA)* I'll talk to her. "Loki and Baldur" by ... ?
NORA: *(Surprised)* Otto Bernick. You'll talk to her ... anyway?
JOHAN: *(Gently)* Anyway. You have a low opinion of us men. I'm sure you have good cause. Let's see now ... *(Playfully he acts this out as if talking to ASTRID)* "Why, Astrid ... you haven't heard of 'Loki and Baldur'? It's the talk of music circles all over Europe. Wherever I go it's 'Loki and Baldur,' 'Loki and Baldur,' 'Loki and Baldur.' Why your arch rival Rosina Gallini is itching to get her vocal chords around it ..."

(NORA is elated and laughs. Orchestra begins tuning.)

CALL BOY: Places!
NORA: I'll pray.
JOHAN: Answered prayers can be the worst kind.
CALL BOY: Places! Places for Act Four.

*(NORA rushes off. JOHAN walks into ASTRID's dressing room.
　　Stage segues into music for the next scene.)*
(Fast fade out.)

(Music Cue 7: The Audition Arrival)

Scene Seven

(On stage.)

(It is night, after a performance of the Opera, chairs set in a semicircle facing a spinet. NORA stands at one side, anxiously. OTTO and the Singers are in a cluster discussing their music. ASTRID's guests are arriving. There are Two Butlers who will be serving from a side table that has been set up.)

ASTRID: *(Being the elegant hostess, to GUESTS)*
GOOD EVENING, MY DEAR –

ARRIVING GUESTS:
GOOD EVENING, GOOD EVENING, GOOD EVENING ...

ASTRID:
SIT DOWN, PLEASE

FIRST GUEST: *(A portly, enthusiastic Woman)*
DEAR ASTRID

(JOHAN enters.)

ASTRID:
AH, JOHAN ...
(Not too pleased)
YOU GOT ME INTO THIS ...

JOHAN:
I GIVE YOU MY WORD ...
A NEW ROSSINI!

ASTRID: *(Laughing)*
DON'T BE ABSURD ...

JOHAN:
REMEMBER ROSINA GALLINI ...

(He goes to greet GUESTS on the opposite side from NORA.)

MORE GUESTS:
GOOD EVENING, GOOD EVENING, GOOD EVENING ...
GOOD EVENING, GOOD EVENING, GOOD EVENING

ASTRID:
SIT OVER THERE ...
(To the BUTLER)
YOU'LL PASS THE WINE
(To the MAID)
YOU'LL PASS THE SALMON ...
(ERIC DIDRICKSON ENTERS. He and ASTRID kiss. Looking around)
IS EVERYONE HERE?
DEAR ERIC
DON'T SLEEP, PLEASE.

GOOD EVENING ...

ERIC: *(Carelessly)*
NOW, ASTRID,
YOU GOT ME INTO THIS
I MAY TAKE A NAP.

(OTTO goes to spinet, followed by the Group of Singers carrying their music.)

OTTO: *(From the piano)*
MADAM, WE'RE READY ...

ASTRID: *(Getting everyone's attention, clapping her hands together)*
CLAP! CLAP!

AND NOW ...
HIGHLIGHTS, I HOPE,
FROM A NEW OPERA ... *LOKI AND BALDUR!*

FIRST GUEST: *(To a Companion)*
THAT'S SO NORWEGIAN!

(OTTO strikes the first stentorian chords of the opera.)

OTTO & CHORUS:
HAY-YAH! H-A-A-A-Y-YAH! HAY-YAH! HAY-YAH!
LOKI AND BALDUR ... BALDUR AND LOKI

(Music Cue 7A: Loki and Baldur – Part I)

MALE LEAD SINGER:
LOKI, GOD OF EVIL!

FEMALE LEAD SINGER:
BALDUR – GOD OF GOOD!

CHORUS:
STRUGGLING FOR SUPREME CONTROL
OVER THE SOUL
OF ... MAN!

FEMALE LEAD SINGER: *(Singing BALDUR)*
NO! LOKI! HEAR ME, NO!
YOUR INFAMIES ARE LEGION!

OTHER WOMAN GUEST:
IT'S SO NORWEGIAN!

NORA: Shhh!

LOKI: *(LEAD MALE SINGER)*
FOOLISH BROTHER! HA HA HA HA HA HA HA!
I WILL SCORCH THE EARTH WITH DROUGHT AND
    FAMINE!

FIRST WOMAN GUEST:
PLEASE PASS THE SALMON

OTTO: *(Talking and playing)* But then, the first rays of the sun return. In an outburst of triumphant transfiguration, Baldur rises, a blessing on his lips for his beloved Norway.

(The "BALDUR" Soprano begins to sing, but OTTO, carried away, takes over and sings in finest castrato style.)

OTTO/BALDUR:
I HAVE RETURNED WITH THE SPRINGTIME
(ASTRID, transfixed, turns and listens to OTTO, smitten by him)
AS THE LONG NIGHT IS FADING
SO I, TOO, AM REBORN ...

(During this, we see JOHAN turn and look at NORA.)
(The scene dims down, in a frozen tableau, leaving a light only on JOHAN and one on NORA, and as he starts to sing, the opera music cuts off.)
(JOHAN looks across the Other People at NORA with compassion and protectiveness.)

JOHAN:
DON'T LOOK SO WORRIED
DON'T BE SO NERVOUS.

(Music Cue 7B: You Interest Me)

I'VE BEEN STUDYING YOUR CASE
HERE'S THE EVIDENCE SO FAR
YOU SEEM WISE
YET YOU'RE NAIVE
YOU'RE CONCEALED
YET YOU'D NEVER DECEIVE
YOU'RE QUESTIONING ...
YET YOU'RE QUICK TO BELIEVE ...
YOU ... INTEREST ME.

(He rises and crosses over towards her. Rest of stage is frozen.)

THERE'S A STORY IN YOUR FACE
WILL IT TELL ME WHO YOU ARE?
YOU LOOK BRIGHT
YET CLOSE TO TEARS,
YOU LOOK BRAVE,
A FACADE FOR YOUR FEARS
YOU SEEM SO STRONG ...
THEN A LOST LOOK APPEARS ...
YOU ... INTEREST ME.

*(He leans against the proscenium, looking searchingly at her still
    face.)*

DID YOU STRANGLE THAT HUSBAND
YOU SIGNED SOMEONE'S NAME FOR
TO GET HOLD OF MONEY
TO SEND HIM AWAY
TO PROLONG HIS LIFE?

ARE YOU ON THE RUN?
ARE YOU STILL HIS WIFE?

(Crossing back – indicating OTTO.)

WILL YOU STAY WITH THIS BUMPKIN
YOU WANT TO WIN FAME FOR
SO YOU EARN THE MONEY
BY SLAVING ALL DAY
TO FULFILL HIS LIFE?
WHEN HIS FAME IS WON
WILL YOU BE HIS WIFE?

FOOLISH MEN!
NOT TO KNOW HOW RARE
IS SOMEONE WHO CAN CARE
THE WAY YOU DO!

(Going back toward his seat.)

I'VE BEEN STUDYING YOUR CASE
AND THE CLUES ELUDE THE CHASE ...
WITH SO MUCH CONFLICTING EVIDENCE
WHAT ARE YOU?
YOU ... ARE SOMETHING NEW
YOU ... INTEREST ME.

(He sits. The lights come up full. The tableau breaks and the action resumes with the singing of the opera.)

OTTO/BALDUR & CHORUS:

(Music Cue 7C: Loki and Baldur – Part II)

(Long held notes.)
LO .... OVE .... AND
FREE .... DOM ....
PEA .... CE .... etc.

(Against the aria the Other singers.)

MAN GUEST:
IT'S SO UTTERLY NORWEGIAN!

FIRST GUEST:
SOMEONE TOOK AWAY THE SALMON ...

ASTRID: *(Suddenly completely captivated)*
ROSSINA GALLINI HASN'T A CHANCE ...
THIS PART IS MINE!

NORA: *(Relieved – exultant)*
THEY'RE QUIET ... THEY'RE LISTENING
THAT LADY'S NOT CARVED IN WOOD ...
MAYBE OUR PRAYERS WILL BE ANSWERED

JOHAN:
MAYBE YOUR PRAYERS WILL BE ANSWERED

NORA:
MAYBE IT *IS* GOOD

JOHAN:
MAYBE IT *IS* GOOD

ASTRID: *(Looking at OTTO, full of desire)*
IF IT CAN BE ARRANGED
AND I THINK IT CAN
THAT YOUNG MAN ... IS MINE!

JOHAN:
BUT BEWARE OF ANSWERED PRAYERS
THEY MIGHT LEAD TO LONELY NIGHTS ...
BEWARE OF ASTRID IN A WIG ... AND TIGHTS ...

(The music swells.)

ALL:
FOREVER!
LIBERTY, FREEDOM ... FOREVER!

*(The FEMALE LEAD SINGER finishes with a tremendously high
note topped by OTTO singing high note over her. She reacts.
NORA starts the applause which ASTRID immediately picks
up and encourages. ERIC who dozed off early on, snores and
wakes with a start.)*

JOHAN: *(Going over to ASTRID)* Well, Astrid, you must
admit the soprano is on-stage a large part of the time.

ASTRID: With me singing it, this role could thrill an
audience!

MAN GUEST: *(To OTTO and the singers)* Congratulations,
young man.

OTTO: Thank you.

(There is general milling and talking.)

ASTRID: Oh, Eric ... you were very naughty. The opera was absolutely –

ERIC: It's whatever you say it is, my sweet. Now, if you'll excuse me, I'll go along and continue my nap. Johan can drop you off.

(He tries to kiss her, she turns away annoyed. He shrugs, amused, exits.)

OTTO: *(With a deep bow to ASTRID, heady with his accomplishment)* Madame Klemnacht ... whatever you thought ... thank you for the great opportunity. I can't tell you what it means to me just to meet you.

ASTRID: *(Intrigued)* You must finish the second act right away ...

NORA: *(Excited)* Oh, Otto, I knew it! You talk to Madame Klemnacht ... I'll get the music together!

(Being diplomatic ... she goes off to the piano ... to put the music together and into a case.)

ASTRID: Mr. Bernick, I would like to hear more about your ideas on this opera, how you visualize it. Let us say ... tomorrow ... at tea time?

OTTO: Yes, yes, of course ... I should be glad to come. Shall I bring the singers?

ASTRID: Oh no. Just you. We can go over the score together ... *(Casually)*. Oh, incidentally, I don't think you need all those political references to Norway and Sweden ... It's too controversial. I'd take them out.

OTTO: *(Immediately)* Of course. It was only an afterthought. The conflict's all there in the music.

JOHAN: *(Dryly)* A young man with the strength of his convictions. *(ASTRID takes a glass of wine for herself and OTTO. They raise glasses together) (Joining NORA)* Well, how do you like your answered prayers so far, Nora?

NORA: *(To JOHAN, quietly, with OTTO and ASTRID a little distance off)* I can't find the words to thank you, Mr. Blecker. But Otto will need a little more to live on ... some evidence that someone believes in his work ...

JOHAN: You mean some kind of ... subsidy?

ASTRID: *(Hears this)* A subsidy!?

NORA: *(To ASTRID)* ... So that he can complete his work ...

OTTO: Nora! She doesn't know what she's saying ...

JOHAN: She has a point, Astrid.

(ASTRID takes in the picture of OTTO and NORA. There is a sudden chill in the air.)

ASTRID: Of course, of course she has. A business discussion is a bit premature in any case. The work shows promise, of course, I'll have to think it over. And tomorrow wouldn't be convenient for me after all. I have fittings all day for Traviata. Well, I've had a really exhausting day!

(She turns abruptly away from OTTO and addresses her GUESTS.)

(Music Cue 8: The Departure)

ASTRID:
GOOD EVENING TO ALL!

OTTO: *(Stunned, trying to talk further)*
BUT ...

GUESTS:
GOOD EVENING, GOOD EVENING, GOOD EVENING ...

ASTRID: *(Taking OTTO's glass away abruptly)*
WE KNOW HOW
TO REACH YOU ...

OTTO:
BUT ...

ASTRID: *(Sailing through)*
AND THANKS TO YOUR LITTLE GROUP

JOHAN: *(Trying to ease the situation)*
SHE'S TRYING TO SAY
SHE DOESN'T KNOW NOW ...

OTTO:
BUT ...

ASTRID:
OH, WHAT A DAY!
(To JOHAN)
DEAR JOHAN,
I WOULD LIKE TO GO NOW ...

OTTO:
BUT ... !

GUESTS:
GOOD EVENING, GOOD EVENING, GOOD EVENING ...
GOOD EVENING, GOOD EVENING, GOOD EVENING ...

ASTRID:
GOOD EVENING TO ALL.

*(JOHAN looks at NORA, shrugs helplessly and follows ASTRID.
The GUESTS go buzzing out as NORA goes to pick up the
music.)*

Scene Eight

*(They all exit. The stage is empty except for OTTO, standing there.
NORA comes toward him carrying the music. He wheels
around – and slaps her.)*

OTTO: *(Furious)* You ruined everything! She loved my
opera until you opened your mouth!

(NORA is stunned.)
(They start walking here – to OTTO's room.)

NORA: We had agreed you would ask for an advance.

OTTO: You talked about money ... and that got us thrown out. My career is finished before it started ... and it's all your fault! What do you know about these things anyway? You should have stayed home and let me handle it myself ... You foolish, silly woman ...

(Stop. They are home.)
(The change to OTTO's room is accomplished with light. The action is continuous.)

Scene Nine

(OTTO's room.)

NORA: I see.

OTTO: I don't see how we can go on together! Trying to eke out a living and thinking of what might have been. It's back to the cafe for me if they'll have me ...

NORA: *(She picks up a letter from the chest)* There's a letter here.

(OTTO grabs it. He starts opening it.)

OTTO: It's from Madame Klemnacht!

(NORA exits.)

(Music Cue 9: A Letter from Klemnacht)

MADAME KLEMNACHT: *(Appears in a light, in another area)*
MY DEAR MISTER BERNICK ...
(OTTO reads, and rereads this phrase ... her voice is sensuous)
MY DEAR ... DEAR ... MISTER BERNICK

ASTRID: *(As OTTO reads)*
I TRIED TO GO TO SLEEP. I LAY AWAKE IN BED ...
THEMES KEPT GOING THROUGH MY HEAD ...
(She sings Baldur's theme, then ...)
I'M SORRY I WAS HASTY ...

(OTTO holds up some money from the envelope.)

OTTO: Look ... fifty kroner! Nora, we're saved! We're
saved!

(He keeps reading.)

ASTRID:
YOU WERE RIGHT ...
YOU ARE AN ARTIST
AND I MUST SHOW FAITH IN YOUR WORK ...
I WILL SUBSIDIZE YOU ... SO YOU CAN CREATE
IN AN ATMOSPHERE OF EASE AND JOY
YOU'RE A TALENTED BOY!

(She exits, trilling.)

OTTO: Nora ... I'm on my way! I found my Princess
Esterhazy! Look! Isn't it wonderful! I didn't mean what I said ...
I was just disappointed. I forgive you! You helped, you silly goose
... you really did ... we did this together!

(NORA re-enters.)

NORA: *(Coldly matter-of-fact)* Since you admit we did it
together, I'll take half the fifty kroner and we're even.
OTTO: But that was for my music. *(Then, indulgently)*
Here's five kroner for the household.
NORA: *(Taking it)* You're very generous. Ten percent is not
bad.

(She goes into the other room.)

OTTO: So everything is all right now ... silly little goose? Nora? ... Nora? ...

(NORA re-enters in bonnet and cape, with bag, and heads for the door.)

NORA: Good-bye, Otto.

(She opens the door and exits. Otto's room goes off.)
(Crossfade to NORA alone in limbo.)

Scene Ten

(Bare stage – limbo – NORA alone.)

(Music Cue 10: Learn To Be Lonely)

NORA:
YOU'VE BEEN CALLED "LITTLE SPARROW"
"LITTLE SKYLARK, LITTLE STARLING"
NOW YOU'VE WORKED YOUR WAY UP TO "LITTLE
    GOOSE," AT LAST!
"LITTLE GOOSE" IS RIGHT.
LOOK AT YOU ...

YOU HAVEN'T DONE WHAT YOU SET OUT TO DO
YOU TRIED TO BUILD A NEW LIFE AROUND ANOTHER
    MAN
STILL TRAPPED IN THE PAST!

(Realizing) Still trapped in the past. *(With clear, sharp resolve)*

MAKE A NEW START!
LIKE A NEW CHICK
SCRATCHING, FIGHTING, CRACKING OUT OF IT'S EGG!
SHAKE YOUR WET FEATHERS DRY
STRAIGHTEN THAT WOBBLY LEG ...

TAKE A SOLITARY STANCE
FOR A SOLITARY DANCE
AND ... LEARN TO BE LONELY!

MAKE A NEW LIFE!
LIKE A NEW STAR
TWINKLING, SPARKLING, BURNING ... GLAD TO BE
    BORN!
SHINE ALONE IN THE SKY!
FEEBLE BUT NOT FORLORN
GETTING BRIGHTER EVERY HOUR
TO A MILLION CANDLE POWER
AND LEARN TO BE LONELY!

WHY DO YOU NEED TO SEARCH FOR A FACE
TO LOOK INTO TO FIND YOUR REFLECTION?
THE WARM KISSES THAT BLANKET THE COLD
CAN'T GUARANTEE PROTECTION ...

WHY BE AFRAID TO WAKE IN THE NIGHT
WITH NO HEAD ON THE PILLOW BESIDE YOU?
WITH NO HAND YOU CAN REACH FOR TO HOLD?
YOUR SECRET SELF MUST GUIDE YOU ...
USE YOUR TIME ALONE TO GROW STRONG
AND DISCOVER THE HIDDEN BEING WITHIN YOU ALL
    ALONG ... !

MAKE A NEW YOU
LIKE A NEW SUN
WHIRLING, SPINNING, ROLLING ... FREE THROUGH THE
    SKIES
LIKE A LONE BUTTERFLY
OPEN YOUR WINGS AND RISE
WORSE THAN BEING ON YOUR OWN
IS TO MATE AND FEEL ALONE

YOU ARE YOUR ONE AND ONLY
LEARN TO LIVE!
LEARN TO BE LONELY!

(She walks off determinedly.)

Scene Eleven

(The Cannery.)
(In Black – music starts.)
(A long table where GIRLS are seated cutting fish. It is ice cold and filthy. The GIRLS are in heavy sweaters, scarves and hats. One GIRL is coughing badly. One place is vacant. The Foreman, MULLER, watches them.)

(Music Cue 11: Rats and Mice [and Fish])

CANNERY GIRLS:
RATS AND MICE ... AND FISH
DIRT AND LICE ... AND FISH
BUT STILL IT'S NICER THAN DAMA HEDWIG'S
COLD WINDS BLOW ... MORE FISH
TIME GOES SLOW ... MORE FISH
BUT ONE STEP LOWER IS DAMA HEDWIG'S

(One of the GIRLS [SELMA] sings the "fish" line solo.)

THROUGH SATURDAY FROM MONDAY
WE DREAM ABOUT SUNDAY
SUNDAY, SUNDAY ...
WE LIVE FOR SUNDAY
WHEN IS SUNDAY

GIRLS:
ISN'T IT SUNDAY YET?
(MORE FISH)
SOAKED AND WET
(LIKE FISH)
BUT STILL IT'S BETTER
THEN DAMA HEDWIG'S

(The singing continues throughout the scene.)
(SELMA stops work in a fit of coughing.)

MULLER: Get to work Selma, this is a herring cannery not a hotel. Where's Nora? This herring barrel's empty.

(A large herring barrel is rolled in by NORA.)

NORA: Sorry, Mr. Muller ... I had to do it alone. Selma has a fever. Feeling any better, Selma?

(SELMA shivers. NORA takes off her scarf and puts it around SELMA.)

SELMA: I've got another job for you, you can roll me home.
NORA: *(She and Another GIRL empty the barrel of fish and spread them on table. NORA takes her seat as they chop away)* Did you see in today's newspaper that the Parliament is allowing women to study mathematics at the University? *(The GIRLS stop chopping, look at her wearily)* No, really ... up till now they thought women's minds couldn't understand higher mathematics.

(In unison, they resume chopping.)

GIRL: *(Sourly, to SELMA)* Tell your friend we don't like it when she talks so superior.
SELMA: *(To NORA)* They don't like it when you talk to superior. *(To the GIRLS)* She doesn't mean any harm. We have this room in Professor Eggleston's house ... He's from the University. That's how Nora got all the books ...
MULLER: Five minutes!

(He exits. The GIRLS stop work and leave the table to stretch themselves. NORA rises. She has been sitting on a stack of books which she puts on the table. She takes a pair of gloves out of her pocket. She puts the gloves on carefully and opens a book. SELMA watches her suspiciously.)

NORA: I promised the Professor I'd wear gloves so the pages won't smell.

SELMA: What did the old boy pick out for you this week?

NORA: *(Holding up books excitedly)* A French philosopher and some books written by women. In England some of the finest novelists are women. George Eliot ... Jane Austin ...

MULLER: *(Entering)* Time's up.

NORA: But it's not five minutes yet!

MULLER: Get to work, Nora!

(The GIRLS go back to chopping herrings. SELMA shushes NORA and tries to get her to sit down.)
(MULLER posts a bulletin on the board.)

GIRLS:	NORA:
RATS AND MICE	
AND FISH	
DIRT AND LICE	*(Looking at the bulletin that's*
AND FISH	*just been posted.)*
BUT STILL IT'S NICER	
THAN DAMA HEDWIG'S	What's this? Seven days a
	week? Sixteen hours a day?
COLD WINDS BLOW	If you don't come in on
(MORE FISH)	Sunday don't bother to
TIME GOES SLOW	come on Monday?
(MORE FISH)	
FISH, FISH, FISH, FISH	**MULLER:**
SUNDAY, SUNDAY ...	Sit down Nora.
WE LIVE FOR SUNDAY	
SAY GOODBY TO SUNDAY	
RATS AND MICE	
(AND FISH)	
DIRT AND LICE –	

NORA: *(With growing anger)* Seven days a week!

GIRLS: *(Hissing)* Troublemaker!

NORA: Sounds reasonable ... Who needs a day off? We'd only get in trouble!

MULLER: Sit down, Nora! Get to work!

NORA: I'd like our employer, Mr. Didrickson to spend one day in this cannery. That French philosopher said "I think, therefore, I am". After one day here, Didrickson would say, "I stink, therefore, I am." Ladies ... Let's walk out. Down with Didrickson! *(MULLER advances on her)* Down with Didrickson! Down with Didrickson! Strike! Strike! Strike!

(SELMA joins in, and then all the GIRLS.)

NORA & ALL THE GIRLS:
Strike! Strike! Strike! Strike! Strike! Strike! Strike! Strike! Strike! Strike! Strike! Strike! Strike!

(This carries on in darkness until the jail scene comes up.)
(Blackout.)

Scene Twelve

(A Prison.)
(A large cell ... and the corridor in front of it. Prostitutes, Criminals, the WOMEN pace like caged animals. NORA is sitting on the floor, writing.)

(Music Cue 12: Jailer, Jailer)

WOMEN:
LOCKED UP FOR STEALING
LOCKED UP FOR BEGGING
LOCKED UP FOR SELLING OUR BODIES IN FRONT OF
    THE CHURCH
LOCKED UP FOR DRINKING
LOCKED UP FOR MARCHING
LOCKED UP FOR STABBING THE BASTARD WHO LEFT
    US IN THE LURCH

LAILER, JAILER, WHILE YOU'RE LOCKING US UP FOR
    LIFE

JAILER, JAILER, WHO'S SAYING HELLO TO YOUR WIFE?

LOCKED UP FOR LOAFING
LOCKED UP FOR WHORING
LOCKED UP FOR MAKING A SPEECH AND DISTURBING
    THE PEACE
LOCKED UP FOR LOOTING
LOCKED UP FOR KNIFING
LOCKED UP FOR OWING THE MONEY WE PAY TO THE
    POLICE

JAILER, JAILER, WHILE YOU'RE LOCKING US UP FOR
    LIFE,
JAILER, JAILER, WHO'S PAYING A CALL ON YOUR WIFE?

NORA: **WOMEN:**
(Writing her letter)
DEAREST CHILDREN ...
DEAREST DARLINGS
I'VE BEEN LEARNING ...
YES, I'M LEARNING

MAMA'S BEEN STUDYING   LOCKED UP FOR
    LAW   STEALING
                            LOCKED UP FOR
                            BEGGING

AND THE LAW IS MORE EQUAL
    FOR SOME THAN OTHERS

                            LOCKED UP FOR
                            DRINKING
                            LOCKED UP FOR
                            MARCHING

WELL, IF THAT IS THE WORLD,
IS IT RIGHT
OR AM I?
IS THE WORLD LOST IN
IGNORANT NIGHT ...
OR AM I?

NORA: *(cont.)*   **WOMEN:** *(cont.)*
                                        JAILER, JAILER, WHILE
                                            YOU'RE LOCKING
                                            US UP FOR LIFE

MAMA'S STILL GOING TO   JAILER, JAILER ...
    SCHOOL
                                        LOCKED UP FOR
                                            LOAFING
                                        LOCKED UP FOR
                                            WHORING

(The JAILER comes across the corridor, followed by JOHAN.)

JAILER: This way, sir ... Here she is, sir ...

(He leads JOHAN in.)

JOHAN: Nora!
NORA: *(Relieved to see him)* Thank you for coming, Mr. Blecker.
JOHAN: Nora! You in jail!
NORA: *(Proudly)* Third time!
JOHAN: *(Upset, looking at the Prostitutes)* What!
NORA: *(Knowing what he must think)* No, no. Making speeches. I had the pleasure of working at Didrickson's Shipping Lines and Fish Canneries! Subhuman conditions! Some day I'm going to meet this Mr. Didrickson and make him see the suffering he's caused!
JOHAN: You've met him already ... twice. First at the cafe on New Year's Eve ...
NORA: *(Remembering)* Oh! The arrogant one! ...
JOHAN: That's Didrickson. And then he was at the audition for Madame Klemnacht ...
NORA: Snoring.
JOHAN: Jailer!

(JAILER goes to JOHAN who presses some money into the JAILER's hand.)

JAILER: Thank you, sir.

(The JAILER unlocks the cell, lets NORA out, locks up again and leaves.)

JOHAN: It's good to see you again, Nora ... Helmer.

NORA: *(Shocked)* You know? Any word of my children?

JOHAN: I can make inquiries if you like.

NORA: I have some letters I've written. If you could manage somehow to get them to their nurse.

(She takes some letters out of her pocket.)

JOHAN: *(Taking them and putting them into his pocket)* Don't worry. I'll see to it.

NORA: Thank you. Now, about this Didrickson.

JOHAN: It's his money that's getting your Otto's opera produced.

NORA: "Loki and Baldur" ... it seems a million years ago.

JOHAN: Yes. Now called by Astrid's request simply "Baldur." I'm invited to his box. *(Suddenly excited) We're* invited to his box for the opening, tonight. *(Acting this out)* "Eric, I am bringing a charming young lady tonight. She is in an absolute fever to meet you and tell you how she feels about you."

NORA: But you're married, Mr. Blecker.

JOHAN: Was.

NORA: Oh, I'm sorry.

JOHAN: No one's fault. Happy ending for both. Well?

NORA: *(Indicating her shabby dress)* In this?

JOHAN: I'll take care of everything.

NORA: When I meet him, may I say anything I like?

JOHAN: If you don't I'll never forgive you.

(He leads her off.)
(As JOHAN and NORA exit, the Jailer music plays. The WOMEN and the prison set go off.)
(In black, music segues from Jailer music to opera music.)

Scene Thirteen

(Music Cue 12A: Jail to Opera Box Transition)

(The Opera House.)

(In Black, there is a burst of opera music. We hear ASTRID singing a portion of Loki and Baldur. This fades out as the lights come up. When the lights come up we see:)

(Downstage is a small salon outside a box, and the door to the box.)

(When the door opens, we see and hear the Opera. When it closes, the opera cuts off.)

(In the salon, there is a table with champagne and glasses.)

(DR. BERG is in the salon. JOHAN enters from the box. When he closes the door, the Opera cuts off.)

JOHAN: *(Entering from a box, crossing and fixing himself a drink)* Good evening Berg.

DR. BERG: You're looking jolly this evening, Blecker.

JOHAN: I love surprises! And tonight I have a fine one for Eric!

(ERIC enters from another box.)

ERIC: Well, Johan – ?

JOHAN: *(With relish)* She's in the box. I'll bring her out presently.

(He goes into the box. A flash of Opera.)

DR. BERG: Astrid's in fine voice. I've heard her relationship with the young composer goes well beyond music.

ERIC: Just her usual infatuation. When I'm ready, I'll hold up a biscuit and make her beg.

(They laugh.)

(The door to the box opens. A flash of Opera.)

(JOHAN comes out with NORA looking beautiful in an elaborate evening gown. ERIC is impressed.)

JOHAN: *(To ERIC)* May I present Miss Nora Nansen. *(To NORA)* Your host, Mr. Eric Didrickson.

NORA: *(Coolly)* How do you do?

ERIC: *(Very much interested)* A pleasure. Champagne, Miss Nansen?

(He pours for her.)

JOHAN: *(To DR. BERG)* Berg, why aren't you inside ... A connoisseur of dance like you?

(He conducts him to the door.)

DR. BERG: But I'm not really ...

(JOHAN pushes him gently inside and closes the door.)

NORA: *(ERIC offers the champagne. NORA refuses it)* Thank you.

(JOHAN gets set to enjoy this.)

ERIC: I thought I knew every beautiful woman in Christiania. Where have you been hiding?

NORA: Most recently in the Prison, before that in the Workhouse, and prior to that, in the worst of them all ... your medieval herring cannery.

ERIC: *(Bantering)* Well, obviously I haven't been going to the right places.

NORA: No, you haven't. You should visit your canneries once in a while. They reveal everything there is to know about you.

ERIC: Oh?

NORA: You're greedy, cruel, you exploit people, you spit on women. You expect human beings to work sixteen hours a day, seven days a week. What more need one know?

ERIC: Don't forget, you've only been admiring me from afar. There's much more. I'm successful. I'm enormously wealthy. I'm a patron of the arts under certain conditions. I'm a splendid dinner companion. And I appreciate a beautiful woman. *(He is standing near her)* Lovely neck.

NORA: Look, I don't belong here. I was in prison for demonstrating against you. Mr. Blecker thought it would be amusing to confront you with one of your working girls. *(Impassioned)* For God's sake, if you value your soul at all, get your foot off the necks of those poor working girls.

JOHAN: *(Applauding and coming over to stand between them)* Bravo, Nora! Now we can enjoy the rest of the opera. Everything's been said that needs to be said!

(He offers his hand to take her inside.)

ERIC: *(Smoothly)* Not quite, old man. Would you mind giving us a few moments privately?

(JOHAN looks questioningly at NORA.)

NORA: *(Staring at ERIC, unexpectedly attracted)* It's all right, Johan.

JOHAN: Oh. Uh ... certainly.

(A bit stiffly, he re-enters the box. A flash of the Opera. The door closes. ERIC comes over to her.)

ERIC: I don't do anything for *God's* sake and my soul is of no value to me, but when *you* demand something ... ah! *(He moves much closer to her)* Make as many demands for changes in the factory as you like, and I will fulfill them all, I promise. In exchange I make only one demand of you ... *(He is right next to her)* Come home with me ... now.

(NORA pulls back.)

NORA: *(Outraged, facing him)* What a detestable creature you are. To try to bargain simple humanity for my poor favors. That's cruel and disgusting! And the answer is "yes!"

ERIC: *(Taken aback)* Yes?
NORA: *(More tentatively, surprised at what she had said)* Yes!

(The door opens and JOHAN stands in the doorway. A flash of Opera.)

    JOHAN: Coming in, Nora?
    ERIC: No.

(NORA shakes her head – "no")

    JOHAN: Oh.

(He hesitates a moment, looking at NORA. She and ERIC are looking directly at each other. JOHAN instantly gets the unexpected picture and, with a resigned nod, withdraws into the box.)
(The door shuts. ERIC comes toward her, standing close. His proximity disturbs her.)

    NORA: *(Rather breathless, feeling the attraction)* Now, the working conditions ... they are ...
    ERIC: Later ...

        (Music Cue 13: Rare Wines)

RARE WINES AND DOWNY PILLOWS
AND CAVIAR ON ICE ...
PERFUMED SHEETS
TURKISH SWEETS
A SATIN GOWN TRIMMED WITH MARIBOU
AND A LOVER WHO KNOWS WHAT TO DO ... WITH
    YOU ...

PINK LIGHT AND SMOKY INCENSE
AND FRAGRANT OILS AND SPICE
WHISPERED SIGHS

HEAVY EYES ...
THE QUICKENED BREATH WHEN THE GAME'S BEGUN
AND A LOVER WHO KNOWS WHEN IT'S WELL DONE ...
    IT'S FUN ...

NORA:	**ERIC:**
I'LL GRIT MY TEETH	DON'T GRIT YOUR TEETH
I'LL CLOSE MY EYES	DON'T CLOSE YOUR MOUTH
I'LL SACRIFICE FOR THE RIGHT	IF YOU DO IT, THEN DO IT ALL
WHAT MATTERS MY LITTLE VIRTUE	WE'LL BITE THE FORBIDDEN APPLE
IF IT WILL WIN THE WORKERS' FIGHT?	LIFE WAS SWEETER AFTER THE FALL ...

ERIC: *(Caressing her)*
WHAT IS YOUR PLEASURE?
(Almost kissing her)
TELL ME YOUR PLEASURE ...

NORA: *(Breathless, pushes away and crosses past him)*
MORE PAY ... AND SHORTER HOURS
A WASH ROOM ON EACH FLOOR
NO MORE LICE
RATS AND MICE
AN HOUR FOR LUNCH AND A BREAK FOR TEA
AND EACH SUNDAY IS A DAY COMPLETELY FREE ...

ERIC:	**NORA:**
	(To herself)
YOU'RE DELICIOUS	THINK OF YOUR MISSION
YOU'RE IRRESISTIBLE	THINK OF THE WORKING GIRLS
	(To him)
	TREAT EACH GIRL AS A LADY
	AND NOT THE FOREMAN'S WHORE

ERIC: *(cont.)*

NORA: *(cont.)*
GIVE THEM HOPE
GIVE THEN SOAP

PERFUMED SHEETS AND
DOWNY PILLOWS
TURKISH SWEETS AND
SMOKY INCENSE

(Facing him determinedly,
trying harder not to give in)
GIVE THEM WOOD
STOVES AND AIR TO
   BREATHE
AND I'M DEMANDING
AN EIGHT HOUR DAY

WE'LL KEEP IT SIXTEEN

NINE

WHAT ABOUT FOURTEEN

TEN

LET'S SAY THIRTEEN

TEN

TWELVE

TEN

TWELVE

(Beginning to weaken)
TEN

TWELVE

TEN

TWELVE

TEN

TWELVE
(Most insinuating)
ELEVEN

TEN
(Giving in to it utterly)
ELEVEN!

(He takes her in his arms. They kiss passionately. Orchestra
Crescendo.)

ERIC:
PURE DELIGHT
ENDLESS NIGHT
THE CURTAINS DRAWN ...

TO DENY THE SUN
AND A LOVER

NORA:
AND A WOMAN

BOTH:
WHO KNOWS WHEN IT'S WELL DONE ...
IT'S FUN ... !

*(They kiss passionately. She initiates it this time. ERIC picks up
    NORA, turns upstage and begins to carry her off upstage as
    we fast fade to black.)*

END ACT I

ACT II

Scene One

(Music Cue 14: Entr'acte)

(Six months later.)
(JOHAN's Office.)
(ASTRID enters in a panic. JOHAN tries to placate her.)

ASTRID: Johan, you've got to help me!

JOHAN: Calm down! Calm down, Astrid!

ASTRID: I've lost him forever!

JOHAN: Oh you know Eric, Astrid. He'll tire of her in no time and ...

ASTRID: Six months! It's never been that long!

JOHAN: Astrid, your throat. You're singing tonight.

ASTRID: Get rid of that girl, Johan ... or I'm getting rid of my lawyer!

(She sweeps out.)

JOHAN: *(Ruefully, to himself)* Six months is a long time ...

(His SECRETARY enters.)

SECRETARY: Excuse me, Mr. Blecker ... that young woman is here to see you again.

JOHAN: Oh yes ... show her in. *(SECRETARY exits ... letting in SELMA, in hat and coat ... nicely dressed)* Yes, Selma, what does your mistress want this time?

SELMA: *(Handing him a bag she is carrying)* Oh, sir ... these are her pearls, sir *(She hands him the bag)* She wants you to take them to the pawn broker ... like you did with the rubies last time. I really wanted to slip one of these pearls off the string ... but

I decided to be grateful. I should be happy she made Mr. Didrickson engage me as her personal maid ... Oh, here's a note.

JOHAN: *(Taking it and reading)* "Dearest Johan ... please invest this in coffee ... it's going up. Are you coming to our house Friday night?" What else have you got there, Selma?

SELMA: Books. I'm in an awful hurry, sir. I have to stop by the Professor's ... return these books for her ... pick up some more ... They'll be missing me at the house, sir ...

JOHAN: Good-bye, Selma ... Tell your mistress I'll be there, Friday.

SELMA: Good-bye Sir ...

(She exits.)

    JOHAN: *(Sings)*

      (Music Cue 15: You Interest Me [Reprise])

I'VE BEEN STUDYING YOUR CASE
ONCE YOU LONGED TO CHANGE THE WORLD
WHAT'S BECOME OF WORKERS' RIGHTS?
WHAT'S BECOME OF THOSE PICKET LINE FIGHTS?
YOU'VE DROPPED IT ALL
FOR YOUR ERIC FILLED NIGHTS.
YOU ... PUZZLE ME.

I'VE BEEN STUDYING YOUR CASE
AND THE CLUES ELUDE THE CHASE
WHO IS THIS NEW YOU?
YOU ... BAFFLE ME.

(Lights fade to black.)

Scene Two

(NORA's bedroom, in ERIC's home.)
(NORA is lying in a sumptuous bed wearing a nightgown, feeling delicious.)

[? *(ERIC is just rising from the bed and going off stage. He kisses her as he leaves.)* ?]

NORA: *(Stretching luxuriously)*

(Music Cue 16: No More Mornings – Introduction)

MAMA REALLY LOVES SCHOOL ... !
LOCKED IN BY PASSION
LOCKED IN BY ARDOR
LOCKED IN BY FEELINGS NOT REMOTELY
CONNECTED TO MY HEAD ...

(ERIC, from the next room, can be heard "la-la-la-ing" vigorously.)

HELD BY HIS KISSING
TRAPPED BY HIS TOUCHING
BOUND LIKE A SLAVE IN THE JUST DISCOVERED
KINGDOM OF HIS BED ...

ERIC'S VOICE:
LA-LA-LA-ETC.

(Music continues under ... NORA lies back stretching. SELMA enters with a breakfast tray.)

SELMA: *(Making fun of her a bit.)* Good morning, "Madame" ... Breakfast.
NORA: Oh, I don't want breakfast yet, Selma.

(She stretches luxuriously.)

SELMA: You'll be late for work at the factory ... The foreman will be mad.
NORA: *(Laughing)* Remember how we dreaded winding up at Madam Hedwig's? Well, look at me, Selma. I'm here ... The awful thing is ... I seem to like it. *(SELMA laughs ... goes to open*

the blinds ...) (Luxuriating) No, no ... leave the curtains drawn ...
Don't let the day in yet! *(SELMA withdraws) (Ecstatic with new-found feelings, like a cat who has lapped up the cream and wants more ... NORA bursts out ... fulfilled, aroused)*

(Music Cue 16A: No More Mornings – Part I)

NO .. MORE ... MORNINGS!
I WANT NIGHT TO STAY ... ON AND ON ...
FILLED WITH MOONBEAMS AND MYSTERY –
WILD ADVENTURING –
PRIVATE RITUALS
ALL OUR OWN!

NO ... MORE ... MORNINGS!
I ORDER THE DAY TO BE GONE ... BE GONE!
KEEP THE LIGHT OUT ...
KEEP THE NIGHT IN ...
IN THE DARK WE CAN SEE
BY THE GLOW OF OUR SKIN

HOLD THE SUNRISE DOWN
SHUT THE SHUTTERS TIGHT ...
NO MORE MORNINGS FOR ME ...
I'VE FALLEN IN LOVE WITH THE NIGHT!

WHO IS THIS SHE
WHO INHABITS MY MIND AND MY BODY?
I CAN'T LIE ...
IT'S JUST ME ...
IT'S THE ME THAT WAS ASLEEP
AND AWAKENED WITH A LEAP!

WHO WOULD HAVE THOUGHT
THERE'S THIS WONDROUS INVENTION ... THE BODY!
OH, NOT I
I WAS TAUGHT
TO PRETEND IT WASN'T THERE ...
BUT IT'S THERE ... OH, GOD, IT'S THERE!

IT'S A TEMPLE
IT'S A PLAYTHING
IT'S THE EYE OF THE STORM
IT'S AN UNDERGROUND SPRING ...

MAKE THE DARKNESS LAST
MAKE THE DAWN TAKE FLIGHT
NO MORE MORNINGS
BATHE ME IN MOONLIGHT
I'M MADLY IN LOVE WITH THE NIGHT!

(She falls back on her pillows ... as ERIC enters "la-la-ing" in his dressing gown.)

ERIC: And how is my lovely little lovebird this morning?

(Going to her ... and kissing her lightly.)

NORA: *(Pulling him down beside her)* Don't go, Eric. Surely your empire can survive for one day without you.

ERIC: That's what they must never find out. I just looked through the company report. With your eleven-hour day, productivity has risen eight percent in the last six months ... Those downtrodden working girls should burn incense in front of your portrait in thankfulness to you.

(Through all this, NORA has been kissing his face.)

NORA: I'm thankful to them.

ERIC: Then we've done rather well out of this.

NORA: The girls could work even better if their fingers weren't frozen. Where are the woodstoves you promised?

ERIC: *(Getting up)* They will be in by next week ... and so will your windows. Now what do you want ... ruby earrings to go with your necklace?

NORA: *(Holding on to him, lightly)* No, I was thinking of a small interest in your business.

ERIC: *(Laughing)* Never. Now, this evening I'm having a small group for billiards, cards and a cold supper. Hugo

Zetterling, a coal giant from Germany, one or two shipping and lumber barons, Nilson, Schmidt, and our ambassador to England, Lars Grunborg. Be particularly charming to him ... I may need him. Here are the names. *(He hands her a sheet of paper)* Memorize them. And wear the black velvet and the pearls.

NORA: I'd prefer the rubies.

ERIC: The pearls ... and there's a new perfume I'm picking up for you. The French woman in the shop recommended it. Wear that.

(He exits.)

NORA: Yes, my emperor ... You've been getting me a lot of perfume lately.

ERIC: *(Offstage)* Oh! More than usual?

NORA: I'd say so. Yes. But whatever I have on isn't doing what it is designed for. You're leaving me to go to work.

ERIC: *(Re-entering, fully dressed now)* I must, Nora, darling. *(Sits on the side of the bed)* What's this?

(Reaches under the bed, picks up some books.)

NORA: Oh, just some reading.

ERIC: Reading?

NORA: *(Caressing him)* The usual silly little romances.

ERIC: *(Reading titles)* "Foreign Market Investments" ... "The History of Money" ...

NORA: *(Playfully)* Very romantic.

ERIC: Machiavelli's "The Prince"?

NORA: *(Flirtatiously)* I'm studying how to overthrow you.

ERIC: Nora, I forbid you to read those books.

(He gets up and starts to leave.)

NORA: It's too late.

ERIC: Now start learning those names, and think up some marvelous new way to wear your hair tonight.

NORA: You're only interested in what's on top of my head, Eric, not what's in it.

ERIC: That's the way it should be. And open up the curtains.

(He goes over as if to open them. NORA jumps out of bed and stops him, throwing her arms around him.)

NORA: No, no ... not yet! *(Holding him around his waist)*

(Music Cue 16B: No More Mornings – Part II)

IT'S A RAINBOW
IT'S A CLOUDBURST
IT'S THE LAST OF THE WINE
IT'S AN UNDYING THIRST!

HOLD THE SUNRISE DOWN
SHUT THE SHUTTERS TIGHT
NO MORE MORNINGS FOR ME
I'VE FALLEN IN LOVE WITH THE NIGHT!

(They embrace. She draws him back to the bed.)
(Fast fade to black.)

Scene Three

(Billiard Room.)
(A billiard table, card table, statues of nudes and chandeliers come on.)
(The GUESTS, all MEN, are in dinner clothes ... There is a MAJOR DOMO and Two BUTLERS in livery and gloves, one of them is OTTO.)

THE MEN: *(ERIC greets them as they enter and as they enter they greet ERIC and each other) (Individual lines sung)*

(Music Cue 17: Transition to Billiards Room)

GOOD EVENING, OLD FRIEND
GOOD EVENING

GOOD EVENING, GOOD EVENING
SO SPLENDID TO SEE YOU
A PLEASURE
YOU'VE PUT ON WEIGHT, OLD MAN
WELL, THANKS, SO HAVE YOU
THE MARKET'S BOOMING ... GOOD
RUMOR IS TRUE
WHAT RUMOR?
A WAR SCARE IS LOOMING ... GOOD
GOOD EVENING, GOOD EVENING, GOOD EVENING,
GOOD EVENING, GOOD EVENING, GOOD EVENING,
GOOD EVENING, GOOD EVENING, GOOD EVENING.

ERIC: *(Calling to OTTO)* Boy! Boy! *(OTTO approaches him)* See if the gentlemen require anything. *(Sarcastically)* You handle that tray very well, Mr. Bernick.

(OTTO bows and goes to the card table with great control. NORA enters, looking resplendent in black velvet, but without the pearls. THE MEN turn and greet her.)

MEN: Ah! Our hostess.
NORA: *(At ease, very much in command)* Gentlemen!
ZETTERLING: Miss Nansen ...
NORA: Oh, dear Mr. Zetterling ... Guten abend und willkomen in Norway!
ZETTERLING: *(Bowing and kissing her hand)* You look ravishing, as always ...
NORA: And you look very pleased with yourself. I just heard Eric say you had completed something quite advantageous ... a coal merger ... was it ... with Kruger and Son? Exactly what is that?
ZETTERLING: *(Patronizingly)* A merger is when two big companies marry, ja? The one with the larger share has the power ... That's the husband, ja?
NORA: Ja.
ZETTERLING: *(Pleased with himself)* Which one will that be, do you think? Kruger or Zetterling? Watch the exchange tomorrow after it is announced.

(They both bow to each other. He goes.)

NORA: *(To SELMA somewhat nervously)* Let me know the minute Mr. Blecker arrives.

(OTTO sees NORA. He approaches her.)

OTTO: Klemnacht dropped me as soon as Didrickson dropped her. He knows I'm here. He hired me.

NORA: That must have given him a great deal of pleasure. *(She sees the AMBASSADOR)* Excuse me. *(She goes to greet him)* Good evening, Ambassador ... How was London?

AMBASSADOR: *(Kissing her hand)* Dreary ... but the Court of St. James is anxious to negotiate for our lumber, so I would say my visit was successful.

NORA: Congratulations. You'll need some big shipping line like Eric's to move all that lumber, I suspect. What on earth do they want it for?

AMBASSADOR: Mass production. Everybody wants everything today. Furniture, sideboards, cupboards, breakfronts, bedposts, pianos, privies ... oh ... I beg your pardon.

(NORA smiles graciously. They bow to each other.)

NORA: Not at all.

(He moves on.)
(NORA is stopped by OTTO.)

OTTO: Nora, I have a new version of my opera. You've got power now. Speak to Didrickson for me. Oh, Nora, I love you still. I'm on my knees.

NORA: *(With a knowing sigh, but not unkindly)* Well, stay that way till get back. *(She goes to ERIC)* Eric, about that extra waiter you hired for this evening ...

ERIC: You mean Bernick? I thought it might amuse you, Nora. And tell him not to bother asking you to intervene. It won't do any good ... I told you to wear the pearls. Go up and put them around that lovely neck of yours at once.

NORA: *(Uneasily)* Oh ... of course, Eric ... in a moment.

(AMBASSADOR joins them.)

AMBASSADOR: Oh, Eric – I'm thinking of recommending your shipping line for government use.
ERIC: Splendid, Your Excellency! How kind!

(As NORA moves away.)

AMBASSADOR: She *is* a charmer.

(They move to the card table. ERIC motions the men to be seated and they begin playing cards.)
(NORA scans the room somewhat nervously. Looks to see if someone has arrived. She passes OTTO.)

NORA: *(Quietly)* He's enjoyed your groveling so much. I think I can convince him to be generous. *(OTTO looks relieved. She sees JOHAN enter. The MEN greet him and continue what they are doing. NORA waves and calls to JOHAN and he crosses to her)* Johan!
JOHAN: *(To NORA, confidentially – no one hears their talk)* I've got them! *(He pats his breast pocket)* That damned pawn broker is in the most out-of-the-way place. *(JOHAN turns to the WAITER nearby)* Here! A whiskey. *(Sees it is OTTO)* Oh ... Sorry ... And sorry about the opera.
OTTO: *(With defiance)* Carmen was a failure when it first opened, too!

(He walks off.)

JOHAN: Poor bastard.
NORA: Thank heavens you got them here. His damned intuition. Why did he want me to wear *them* of all things?
JOHAN: It was unnecessary to put us both through this. I told you you didn't have to pawn anything else.
NORA: *(With relish)* I'm greedy. I don't want to sell any of

my stocks yet. *(Looking over at ERIC)* I'll put them on in the hall. Leave them in the umbrella stand.

ERIC: *(Playing the card game)* Play the diamond.

AMBASSADOR: Play your own game, Eric.

JOHAN: *(To NORA)* No. I'll put them on you here.

NORA: *(Nervously)* Suppose he sees?

JOHAN: *(Edgily)* Suppose he does. I've been playing your game. Play mine for a change.

ZETTERLING: *(At card table)* And then I could not remember which was trump.

NORA: Please hurry!

(He puts the pearls around her neck. ERIC, on the other side of the room, does not notice. NORA is relieved.)

JOHAN: Well, greedy one. You had another good day on the exchange.

NORA: Yes?

JOHAN: The coffee market was good to you. Ten points profit.

ERIC: *(As that round of cards is won)* Good man!

NORA: Invest half in Mr. Zetterling's coal first thing in the morning. He told me he just merged with Kruger.

(She says this smiling, as if having trivial chit-chat as ERIC joins them. He sees the pearls.)

ERIC: Ah, you've put them on.

NORA: *(With mock innocence)* Why, did you think I had pawned them? I know they're not mine. They're yours. One possession showing off another.

ERIC: And beautiful, too.

(He touches the pearls and walks off.)

JOHAN: *(Stiffening)* You've gotten very sure of yourself.

(She looks searchingly at JOHAN a moment.)

KLOSTER: *(KLOSTER gets up from the card table)* Miss Nansen.

NORA: *(To JOHAN, still looking searchingly at him)* Forgive me. *(NORA turns away from JOHAN)* Mr. Kloster?

KLOSTER: By popular vote at this table, the gentlemen have decided that you are to join us at whist.

NORA: *(Asking permission)* Eric?

ERIC: *(Near the card table)* Yes, by all means play, my dear.

(She goes to the table. The MEN rise to greet her. She sits and starts to play.)

JOHAN: *(OTTO brings JOHAN his whiskey. JOHAN downs it in a gulp and crosses to ERIC, obviously tense and upset by his feelings and his last encounter with NORA)* Come on, Eric I'll beat you at billiards. *(They go to the billiard table, choose cues. JOHAN is now very tense. He drinks during the game, impatiently)* Come on, I'll start. *(He shoots)*

(During the game, OTTO is near the billiard table with his tray of drinks from which JOHAN will keep taking glasses of whiskey and onto which he puts his emptied glasses of whiskey.)

ERIC: You seem a bit agitated, old man.

(JOHAN looks over at NORA. ERIC follows and looks also. OTTO, with his tray, also looks at her.)

JOHAN: Come on! *(He is about to shoot, then stops. Longingly)*

(Music Cue 17B: There She Is)

THERE SHE IS ...

OTTO: *(To himself, hopeless)*
THERE SHE IS ...

ERIC: *(Confident, chalking cue)*
THERE SHE IS ...

JOHAN: *(Sardonically)*
YES, I KNOW I ARRANGED IT
I THOUGHT IT AMUSING
TO THROW YOU TOGETHER
BUT HOW I'VE REGRETTED IT EVER SINCE ...
WHEN YOU CATCH HER EYE
HOW IT MAKES ME WINCE ...

ERIC:
REALLY, JOHAN, I NEVER SUSPECTED

JOHAN:
I WAS PUZZLED, INTRIGUED,
THEN ATTRACTED ... I FOUND HER
SO DIFFERENT ... OUR PATHS
KEPT ON CROSSING, AND I
TRIED TO HELP HER OUT,
NOT QUITE KNOWING WHY ...
NOW I HAVE NO DOUBT ...
THERE SHE IS ...

OTTO: *(To himself)*
THERE SHE IS ...

ERIC:
THERE SHE IS ...

OTTO: *(To himself)*
THERE SITS MY NORA
REMEMBER ME, NORA!

JOHAN:
FOOLISH MAN,
FEELING LIKE A CHILD
LEFT OUTSIDE A WINDOW FULL OF TOYS

ERIC: *(Taking billiard shots)*
LA LA LA ... LA LA LA LA ...

JOHAN:
AND THERE'S NO USE CRYING
THERE'S NO USE PRESSING MY FACE
AGAINST THE WINDOW PANE

ERIC:
IS THIS YOU, JOHAN, THE URBANE?

JOHAN:
HUNGRY MAN, TEMPTED AND BEGUILED
BY A FEAST ANOTHER MAN ENJOYS ...

ERIC:
LA LA LA ... LA LA LA LA ...

JOHAN:
AND THERE'S NO USE REACHING
THERE'S NO USE LONGING
FOR SWEETS I NEVER CAN ATTAIN ...

OTTO:
LOOK AT ME, NORA ...

ERIC:
I'M AMUSED TO SEE YOU LIKE THIS, OLD FRIEND
CHILDISHLY OUT OF CONTROL
TEARING YOUR HAIR
BEATING YOUR BREAST.

THE WORLD IS AWASH WITH WOMEN ...
AIM AT SOME OTHER GOAL
AND KINDLY REMEMBER
YOU'RE MY GUEST.

OTTO: *(To himself)*
THERE SHE IS ...

ONCE SHE WAS MINE ...
IT MAKES ME ILL ...
IF I HAD BEEN A LITTLE SMARTER
SHE WOULD BE MINE STILL.

JOHAN:
THERE SHE IS ...

OTTO: *(To himself)*
THERE SHE IS ...

ERIC:
THERE ... SHE ... IS ...

OTTO: *(To himself)*
THINK OF ME, NORA ...
SPEAK TO HIM, PLEAD FOR ME
GET HIM TO SPONSOR ME, NORA ...

JOHAN:
PASSIVE MAN ...
LOST AND GOING WILD
WITH A HEART AND
HEAD FILLED UP WITH NOISE ...

JOHAN:	**ERIC:**
TORN BY BASE EMOTIONS	LA, LA, LA ...
LIKE RAGE AND ENVY	LA, LA, LA, LA ...
FOR SHE IS OUT OF REACH,	
JUST BEYOND MY TOUCH,	
STILL WITHIN MY SIGHT ...	
BUT WHAT'S THE USE?	
SHE'S YOURS, YOU SWINE ...	

ERIC: Watch out, old man, one of these days you'll go too far.

JOHAN: Would smashing you in the face be going too far?

ERIC: Really, Johan.

(JOHAN slams his billiard cue down on the table. ERIC laughs. JOHAN goes toward the door, stops and looks back at NORA.)

OTTO:
THERE SHE IS ...

ERIC:
THERE SHE IS ...

JOHAN:
THERE SHE IS ...

OTTO:
ONCE SHE WAS MINE

ERIC:
NOW SHE'S MINE

JOHAN:
AND SHE'LL NEVER BE ...
MINE ...

(He dashes out.)
(Unaware of all this, suddenly NORA jumps up from the table.)

NORA: *(Exultant)* I won! I won! How exciting! I won!
MEN: *(Ad lib)* Bravo!
ERIC: How does it feel, my dear?
NORA: *(Heady)* I think I feel the way you feel all the time!

(Counting money, feeling very high; carried away with herself.)

(Music Cue 17C: Power)

I LOVE THE SMELL OF IT
THE SOUND OF IT
POWER, POWER

I FEEL IT LIKE A MOTOR IN THE ROOM
BOOM BOOM BOOM
IT GOES WITH THE SMELL OF BRANDY
THE SMELL OF CIGARS
OF MEN'S COLOGNE
IT GOES WITH THE SOUND OF CASUAL BARITONE
    RUMBLINGS,
LOW CONSPIRATORIAL WHISPERS

THE CLICK OF BILLIARD BALLS,
THE SLAP OF PLAYING CARDS
IT'S GONE TO MY HEAD
I WANT SOME OF MY OWN!

I LOVE THE FEEL OF IT
THE LOOK OF IT
POWER, POWER
ELECTRIC CHARGES FILL THE ROOM WITH FIZZ
ZIZZ ZIZZ ZIZZ ZIZZ
IT GOES WITH THE FEEL OF SILVER
THE CRACKLE OF CASH
THE WEIGHT OF GOLD
IT GOES WITH THE LOOK OF SNOWY-WHITE
BILLOWING SHIRTFRONTS
BLACK MEPHISTOPHELIAN WHISKERS
THEY TELL ME TO BE
CONTROLLING, NOT CONTROLLED

THE FLASH OF A CUFFLINK
A RUFFLED CUFF ...
PUFF PUFF PUFF PUFF
PUFF PUFF PUFF PUFF

WHAT GIVES YOU POWER?
THE LION'S SHARE –
WHAT GIVES YOU POWER?
THE HIGHEST BID –
MASS PRODUCTION

MERGE THE COAL MINES
SHIP THE LUMBER
BUILD A PRIVY
PEOPLE WANT AND PEOPLE BUY
SO PEOPLE SELL AND STOCKS GO HIGHER ...
WHAT GIVES YOU POWER?

NOT PLAYING FAIR –
WATCH PROFITS FLOWER
FROM DIRT YOU DID –
STUDY HIST'RY
SHAPE THE FUTURE
BUY A STATESMAN
SELL A CANNON
GERMANY AND FRANCE WANT MORE,
SO SELL TO BOTH AND START A WAR.

PUFF PUFF PUFF PUFF
BANG BANG BANG BANG.

I LOVE THE TASTE OF IT
THE SENSE OF IT
POWER, POWER
IT'S MAN TO MAN AROUND A SMOKE-FILLED ROOM ...
BANG, ZIZZ, BOOM!

I WATCH YOU HUFF AND PUFF
AND CALL EACH OTHER'S BLUFF
EACH ONE PROTECTING HIS
I KNOW WHAT POWER IS
TAKING, WINNING
USING, GOUGING
GRABBING WHAT YOU CAN
BEING BORN A MAN!

(There is tension when she finishes.)

  ERIC: Gentlemen, a light repast will be served inside. *(The*

MEN start going off. NORA starts to go along, too) Good night, Nora.

(NORA stops. The MEN continue off.)

    NORA: *(Uneasily)* I will – see you later?
    ERIC: *(Coldly)* I think not. I'll be sleeping in my private chambers. Goodnight, Nora.

(He leaves to follow the MEN off. NORA is left alone as the lights fade to black.)

Scene Four

(A hallway.)
(It is the next morning.)
(NORA enters in a negligee.)
(A MAID enters from the other side with breakfast tray.)

    NORA: Good morning.
    MAID: *(Uncomfortably)* Good morning, Madam. It's only eight o'clock ... you're up early ...
    NORA: Is that for Mr. Didrickson?
    MAID: *(Flustered)* Yes, I was taking it up to him ...
    NORA: That's what I got up for. I'll take it. Thank you.
    MAID: Oh, it's no trouble, Madam. Let me.
    NORA: I want to surprise him.

(NORA tries to take the tray, but the MAID backs away, panicked.)

    MAID: *(Anxiously)* Please, Madam ...

(A YOUNG WOMAN comes in from the direction of ERIC's bedroom in street clothes.)

    YOUNG WOMAN: Oh! Pardon! ... I am lost ... so many hallways ...

(She has a French accent.)

    NORA: *(Shocked to see her)* Oh?
    YOUNG WOMAN: I am looking for ze door.
    NORA: "Ze" door to what?
    YOUNG WOMAN: To ze outside ... to ze street.
    NORA: *(Her suspicions growing)* Do you by any chance work in a perfume shop?
    YOUNG WOMAN: Yes. The gentleman of the house asked me to deliver a new scent we have.
    NORA: At eight in the morning?
    YOUNG WOMAN: I am going. Goodbye.

(She looks for an escape. NORA stops her from going.)

    NORA: Just a minute. How dare you! This is *my* house!
    YOUNG WOMAN: *(Defiantly)* Is it? I came by invitation.
    NORA: *(Livid)* I don't believe it. *(Calling)* Eric! Eric!
    YOUNG WOMAN: It's true! Ask him ... he's awake. I just left him five minutes ago.
    NORA: ERIC!

(By this time ERIC has entered in his dressing gown.)

    ERIC: What's all this noise? *(Sees YOUNG WOMAN)* Oh my God!
    NORA: *(Blazing)* Did you ask this woman here?
    ERIC: Jacqueline, go home!
    NORA: JACQUELINE!

(She emits an animal-like noise, leaps at ERIC and starts pummeling him.)

    ERIC: Nora ... Nora ... Stop it!

(Holds her hands.)

    JACQUELINE: Never have I been so humiliated! You told me she was away!

(She runs out.)

ERIC: Nora! Calm yourself. It's nothing!

NORA: *(Exploding)* Nothing!? You monster! How could you do this! Here! In my own house!

ERIC: *(Imperiously)* May I remind you it is my house.

NORA: *(Suddenly crumbling)* Eric! Eric! I can't share you! I won't!

(Trying to hold on to him.)

ERIC: *(Pulling away)* Don't be so foolish, Nora.

NORA: *(Weeping, hurling herself at him)* Am I not enough for you? Eric! Eric! *(She sinks weeping abjectly to the floor at his feet)* I never knew I could feel this way? I can't live without you!

ERIC: Nora, come to your senses!

NORA: *(Crying)* You can't treat me like this!

ERIC: *(He stands over her menacingly)* Can't I? ... Last evening if you recall, you referred to yourself as a possession of mine. I don't think you really meant that. Those were just words to you ... But you must realize that this is so. You are here only by my sufferance ... because I want you.

NORA: *(Stopping her crying, with realization)* I see.

ERIC: I'm not saying the time won't come when I won't want you, but I do now.

NORA: *(Composing herself)* Thank you, Eric.

ERIC: But not the way you are this minute ... Messy ... like a crushed bird run over by a carriage wheel. I want you decorative ... amusing ... compliant. Now get up, and I don't want to see you until you are ready to be all three of those things.

NORA: *(Softly)* Yes, my Emperor. *(She gets up slowly, straightens up and calls out, firmly)* Selma, Selma ... bring me my new coat and hat.

ERIC: Where do you think you're going?

NORA: *(With full realization)* I'm not sure. But I know where I've been. Eric – *(She walks over to him)* messy as I am, would you please touch my lovely neck?

(Music Cue 18: Touch My Neck)

(ERIC now amused, runs his fingers along the side of her neck.)

ERIC: Well ... !

NORA: Nothing. Good. I'm cured. *(SELMA comes in with the coat and hat ... NORA takes them. SELMA exits)* Thank you ... thank you, Eric, for waking me from my long perfumed dream. And thank you for the temporary use of your jewels ... Among other things they made this coat and hat possible ... They're mine ... earned ... and that's all I'm taking with me.

(During this she is hiking up her peignoir and pulling her coat on over it and putting on her hat.)

ERIC: What do you think you're doing? You can't go ... I won't let you. I forbid it.

(He approaches her threateningly.)

NORA: I know you can stop me, Eric. You're bigger and stronger. One blow with that fist would do it. But you'd have what you don't want ... a crushed bird ... and a frigid one. *(She pulls off earrings, puts them in ERIC's hand)* Goodbye, Eric.

(She starts for the door.)

ERIC: *(Suddenly reappraising her)* Stay, Nora ... Perhaps you're the one woman I would not get tired of.

NORA: I can't wait around to find out.

(She goes out and slams the door.)
(Blackout or crossfade to NORA alone in limbo.)

Scene Five

(NORA appears, very resolute and clear.)

NORA:
DEAREST CHILDREN ...
DEAREST DARLINGS ...
MAMA HAS STUDIED HERSELF

(Music Cue 19: Transition to Grand Cafe)

THOUGH SHE HOPED SHE WOULD ALWAYS BE OPEN
    AND HONEST
SHE DISCOVERED SHE COULD   BE DECEITFUL AND
    SELFISH ...
AND WHEN YOU LOSE YOUR WAY
IT'S LIKE DROWNING IN A POOL ...
AND THE WORST OF DEPENDENCE IS NOT TO HAVE
    MEANS
TO CONTROL YOUR OWN LIFE YOU HAVE GOT TO HAVE
    MEANS
THAT YOU PUT TO WORK LIKE A USEFUL TOOL

(Spoken) Mama's still going to school.

(As NORA goes off, crossfade to another area – in limbo –)
(JOHAN enters, looking elegant, reading a note.)

JOHAN:
"DEAREST JOHAN ... I MUST SEE YOU.
HOW I'VE MISSED YOU ... HOW I NEED YOU!

(Spoken) Meet me today, ... at the Grand Cafe ..." *(Exuberant)*

(Music Cue 19A: At Last)

AT LAST! SHE CAN SEE ME AS A MAN ... AT LAST!
AT LAST ... I'M NO LONGER SIMPLY PART OF HER
PLAN TO INVEST, TO EXPAND, TO ACQUIRE ...
AT LAST ... I CAN HOLD HER HAND, NOT HER PURSE ...
AND SPEAK, NOT IN SUMS ... BUT IN VERSE!
AT LAST ... THERE'LL BE KISSES AS WE LAUGH

ABOUT THE WAY THIS ALL BEGAN
AT LAST ... SHE SEES ME ... SHE LOVES ME AS A MAN!

(Fast fade out.)

Scene Six

(The Christiania Restaurant – Indoors.)

SUMMER

(The PATRONS have filled the stage. There are Waiters, etc. Champagne and chandeliers come in. There is only one table on-stage, used by the Principals.)

(Music Cue 20: Power Comments – Part I)

PATRONS:
WHAT GIVES YOU POWER
THE LION'S SHARE
WHAT GIVES YOU POWER
NOT PLAYING FAIR

POWER, POWER
YOU FEEL IT LIKE A MOTOR IN THE ROOM
BOOM! BOOM! BOOM!

(They freeze in an elegant post. NORA enters, in simple street attire. JOHAN enters from the other side.)

(Music Cue 20A: Cafe – Summer)

JOHAN: *(Rushing to her)* Nora, at last!

(She gives him a friendly embrace.)
(He is disappointed.)

NORA: *(Moving to table)* At last! How I've missed you! *(She leads him to the table and they sit)* Johan, how much money have I got?

JOHAN: Enough. Plenty.

NORA: And it's all in your name.

JOHAN: *(Laughing)* Don't you trust me?

NORA: Of course. I just don't know if you'll approve of what I'm going to do with it. A perfume shop. Dear Johan. Forgive the rush but we'll lost the shop unless I sign the lease today.

JOHAN: *(A little taken aback)* Lease? Shop?

(A Waiter has brought champagne in a bucket.)

NORA: *(Who has been looking toward the entrance at the side)* Jacqueline! *(This is not what JOHAN had expected. JACQUELINE comes to the table)* Jacqueline LeBeau ... Here he is ... Johan Blecker.

JACQUELINE: *(Surprised)* No! I pictured a kindly, white-haired old gentleman. How do you do?

JOHAN: *(Wryly)* How do you do? *(He realizes she is staying)* Won't you sit down?

NORA: *(Taking papers from her bag)* Jacqueline and I found we had an interest in common ...

JOHAN: Oh?

NORA: *(Spreading papers out on table)* And her father's perfume shop is for sale. I know I can make it work, Johan ... but ...

JOHAN: But ... you can't own it in your own name ... so ...

NORA: Exactly ... *(Looking at him anxiously)* Johan ... would you ... ?

JOHAN: *(He nods ... resigned, disappointed)* I'll take care of everything.

NORA: *(Leaving the papers for JOHAN ... hurrying)* Thank you! *(NORA gets up)* Jacqueline, they're waiting for us! *(Suddenly concerned)* Johan, am I using you?

JOHAN: *(Still wry)* Yes, but to be useful to someone you care about ... a friend.

(The Waiter has brought the check.)

NORA: Let me!
JOHAN: *(Firmly)* Nora! *(He takes the check)* It must be nice to know you can. But, even *I* am not ready for this yet.
NORA: Thank you again, dear Johan. Jacqueline, come!

(She and JACQUELINE get their things together and go. The Waiter starts to pour the remaining champagne in JOHAN's glass.)

JOHAN: *(Stopping him)* I think I need something stronger than that. Bring me a ... *(He cuts off, then, bitterly)* Never mind!

(He pays the check and goes out in the opposite direction. The Patrons swirl and change positions.)
(Music and Patrons as Segue.)

(Music Cue 20B: Power Comments – Part II)

WHAT GIVES YOU POWER
THE HIGHEST BID
WHAT GIVES YOU POWER
THE DIRT YOU DID

POWER, POWER
THE MORE YOU GET YOU NEVER HAVE ENOUGH
PUFF, PUFF, PUFF, PUFF.

(The Patrons exit.)
(NORA's table is now L. of C. NORA, JACQUELINE enter from side in different, rich attire. They cross to the table and sit. The Waiter comes over and pours champagne as JOHAN enters hurriedly, also in other attire, looking elegant.)

JOHAN: *(Carrying papers)*
I'M LATE – I HAVE JUST A MOMENT MORE
I'M LATE ... LADIES, NOW YOU OWN A MUCH LARGER STORE ...

IT'S ALL YOURS, IT'S ALL CLEAR ... IT'S ALL SIGNED!

(They are excited and start reading the papers.)

(Spoken) but from now on, the signing will be done by Rolf Thommassen ... an associate in my office ... very capable fellow ... he'll take over everything. But be careful ... the company's not in profit yet.

JACQUELINE: *(Concerned)* We can't get materials for less.

NORA: *(Off-hand, busy with papers)* Simple ... Cut the girls' wages a little.

JOHAN: *(Amused)* Those poor working girls ... ?

(Music Cue 20C: Cafe – Autumn)

NORA: *(Appalled at what she has said)* What's happening to me? I don't think I like myself at the moment. *(She stops ... an idea)* Wait ... I have an idea! If I *have* to reduce the wages for awhile, in exchange I could give them each a small share in the business ...

JOHAN: So as the company grows ... It might work ...

NORA: Oh, I know this will work!

JOHAN: *(Getting ready to go)* Good! I'll have Thommassen start drawing up the papers ...

NORA: *(This is starting to sink in)* Thommassen? *(Realizing he's leaving)* But why the rush? Business appointment?

JOHAN: Previous engagement.

(A beautiful, sumptuously dressed Woman enters. JOHAN goes to greet her.)

NORA: *(To JACQUELINE)* That actress?

CAMILLA FORRESTER: Johan!

JOHAN: *(Presenting her)* Camilla Forrester. Miss Nansen, Miss Le Beau.

CAMILLA: How do you do?

NORA: But, Johan, we haven't finished discussing the lease ...

(He is leading CAMILLA to another table R. of C.)

JOHAN: Nora, you can walk perfectly well by yourself by now. Remember, Rolf Thommassen!
NORA: Don't keep saying that!
JOHAN: Ladies –

(JOHAN and CAMILLA go to the table. NORA is sitting with her back to them. JACQUELINE half-facing them.)

JACQUELINE: *(Looking through things)* We're really doing better, you know. The Royal Princesses'
ladies-in-waiting come in ... and the Prime Minister's wife ... and Astrid Klemnecht wants four bottles delivered to her dressing room ...

(Music Cue 20D: There He Is)

NORA: *(Ruefully)*
THERE HE IS ...

JACQUELINE:
THERE HE IS
ONCE HE WAS YOURS
IT MAKES YOU ILL
IF YOU HAD BEEN A LITTLE SMARTER,
HE WOULD BE YOURS STILL ...
THERE HE IS.

NORA: *(As casually as possible)* *(Spoken)* Anything fascinating going on at that table?

(At the other table, JOHAN is attentive to CAMILLA. JACQUELINE describes what they are doing.)

JACQUELINE: Not really ... Oh ... he's pouring champagne in her glass ... then in his ... he's tasting hers ... then passing it to her ... Oh, my God! They're doing that silly old thing ... I can't believe it ... !

NORA: What? Doing what?

JACQUELINE: *(Acting this out)* Oh, you know ... that foolish thing where they link elbows ... and ... Oh! She spilled hers ... all over him!

NORA: Good. He must be furious.

(JOHAN is discreetly drying the spilled wine from her bosom with a napkin.)

JACQUELINE: He seems to like it. Some got on her ... Oh! He's holding her ... Now he's licking it off her ...

NORA: Off her what ... ?

JACQUELINE: Her wrist. Oh, they've called the waiter ... He's getting the bill ... Just a sip of champagne and away ... ! They're leaving ...

(They pass their table.)

JOHAN: Ladies.

(JOHAN and CAMILLA exit.)

NORA: *(Sings)*
THERE HE IS ...

JACQUELINE:
THERE HE IS ...

NORA:
TOO LATE ...

(NORA runs out.)

JACQUELINE: Nora!

(JACQUELINE follows.)
(The PATRONS enter at the scene change.)

(Music Cue 20E: Power Comments – Part III)

PATRONS:
WHAT GIVES YOU POWER
THE LION'S SHARE
WHAT GIVES YOU POWER
NOT PLAYING FAIR

POWER, POWER
YOU FEEL IT LIKE A MOTOR IN THE ROOM
BOOM! BOOM! BOOM!

(The PATRONS exit.)
(From opposite sides, NORA and JOHAN enter.)
(The table is now DSC.)
(Sung)

(Music Cue 20F: I'm Making Love To You – Part I)

JOHAN:
WELL, NORA ...

NORA:
DEAR JOHAN ...

JOHAN:
YOU'RE LOOKING WELL ...

NORA:
YOU'RE LOOKING WONDERFUL! IT'S BEEN SO LONG ...

JOHAN:
YES, THREE MONTHS ...

NORA:
THREE MONTHS. I'VE JUST COME BACK FROM ...

BOTH:
STOCKHOLM

JOHAN:
YES, THOMMASSEN'S BEEN TELLING ME ... THE NEW STORE ...

NORA:
YES, THE NEW STORE IN STOCKHOLM ...

(Music stops. They look at each other ... Uncomfortable pause.)

JOHAN: Well, let's sit down ... shall we? *(They sit. A Waiter comes over)* Tea, please. *(The Waiter nods and exits.) (Music under)* Well, Nora ... what next? Another store?

NORA: No, I'm going to sell all of them. *(JOHAN is surprised)*

(Music Cue 20G: I'm Making Love To You – Part II)

(Singing)
THE BUSINESS GAVE ME WHAT I NEED ...
I HAVE MY INDEPENDENCE.
BUT SELLING PERFUME'S NOT THE WAY
I'LL USE MY INDEPENDENCE ...
I'LL START A SCHOOL ...
I'LL START ... A WOMEN'S SCHOOL
WHERE GIRLS CAN LEARN ... AND CHANGE THEIR LIVES.

JOHAN: Bravo, Nora! *(Looking at her)* You *are* looking well ... *(Singing to himself)*

MAY I SAY YOU'RE LOOKING WELL ...
NEVER SAW A NICER DAY ...
HAVE YOU SEEN THE LATEST PLAY?
THE NEW CAFE?
THE SHOPS ALONG THE WAY?

I MAY SAY IT LOOKS LIKE RAIN ...
BUSINESS HAS BEEN GOOD THIS YEAR ...

YET, THE MARKET'S DOWN, I FEAR
BUT, OH, MY DEAR
CAN'T YOU HEAR?
I'M MAKING LOVE TO YOU!

(The tea has been brought, JOHAN pours.) Sugar?

NORA: Two, please.

JOHAN: *(As he serves)*
I'M PICTURING US ALONE SOMEWHERE
I'M KISSING YOUR MOUTH
STROKING YOUR HAIR ...
TELLING YOU I LOVE YOU
ASKING DO YOU LOVE ME?
LOVE ME ... PLEASE, LOVE ME!

(To NORA) Some cake, Nora?

(He passes it.)

NORA: Thank you.

(Enter ERIC with two young ladies.)

ERIC: Good afternoon ...
NORA & JOHAN: Eric ...
ERIC: May I present my two "nieces" ... Berta and Birgit?

(They nod and exit.)

NORA: But, what about you, Johan? ... Is Camilla? ... Do you
see Camilla?

JOHAN: Uh ... well. Yes. *(Singing)*
CAMILLA'S TOURING NOW,
SHE'S PLAYING NEXT IN COPENHAGEN
I'M OFF TO TAKE THE TRAIN

TO SEE HER PLAY IN COPENHAGEN
THESE PAST THREE MONTHS
I'VE GONE TO EVERY TOWN
TO MEET HER THERE WHEN SHE ARRIVES ...

NORA: *(Wryly)* Bravo, Johan. *(Wistfully)* Well, it seems to agree with you ... You're looking well ...

NORA: *(Singing to herself)*
I MAY SAY YOU'RE LOOKING WELL
NEVER SAW A NICER DAY
I MAY SPEAK OF WHAT'S AHEAD
THE LIFE I'VE LED
AND WHAT I'LL DO INSTEAD ...

I MAY SAY IT LOOKS LIKE RAIN
YET, WHO KNOW, IT STILL MIGHT CLEAR
BUT BENEATH THIS THIN VENEER
OH, MY DEAR ...
CAN'T YOU HEAR?
I'M MAKING LOVE TO YOU!

JOHAN: More tea?
NORA: I think not, thank you ...
OTTO: *(OTTO approaches the table in elegant clothes and on his arm is a Dowager)* Good afternoon ...
NORA: Why, Otto ...
OTTO: I have a new version of my opera ... I do hope you will come to the opening ...

(He hands them tickets.)

NORA & JOHAN: Thank you, Otto.

(OTTO and the Dowager exit.)

JOHAN: Well, at least she smells nice.
NORA: One of ours ...

JOHAN: *(Laughing)* Should we go?

(Holding up the opera tickets.)

NORA: *(Serious)* Johan, I'm taking a train, too ... back home ...

JOHAN: *(Alarmed)* What! You're not going back to Torvald!

NORA: No, I'll never do that. But I want to talk to him, face to face ... tell him how I've changed, and ask him to share the children with me.

JOHAN: Nora, when you left, you gave up all right to the children.

NORA: I know. But maybe by this time, he has changed, too ... Johan, I have to face him, and try.

JOHAN: *(Attempting to be jocular)* Be careful, Nora. A cold Norwegian night ... who knows what might happen ... old feelings might get stirred up ...

NORA: Oh never, Johan, never.

(Music under stops.)

JOHAN: Shall I get the bill? *(NORA nods)* Waiter!

(He is right there.)
(JOHAN looks at the bill.)
(JOHAN and NORA look out front and sing together, but not to each other.)

BOTH: *(Singing. Song divided between them ... with answers, harmonies, etc.)*
I MAY SAY YOU'RE LOOKING WELL ...
NEVER SAW A NICER DAY ...
HAVE YOU SEEN THE LATEST PLAY?
THE NEW CAFE?
THE SHOPS ALONG THE WAY?

I MAY SAY IT LOOKS LIKE RAIN
BUSINESS HAS BEEN GOOD THIS YEAR

YET THE MARKET'S DOWN, I FEAR
BUT, OH, MY DEAR
CAN'T YOU HEAR
I'M MAKING LOVE TO YOU!

I'M PICTURING US ALONE SOMEWHERE
I'M KISSING YOUR MOUTH ...
STROKING YOUR HAIR ...
TELLING YOU I LOVE YOU
ASKING DO YOU LOVE ME? LOVE ME ... PLEASE LOVE
    ME!

I MAY SAY YOU'RE LOOKING WELL ...
NEVER SAW A NICER DAY ...
BUT NO MATTER WHAT I SAY
OH, MY DEAR
CAN'T YOU HEAR
I'M MAKING LOVE TO YOU!

(Music cuts off.)
(The Waiter comes back. JOHAN pays him.)

JOHAN: Uh ... *(Uncomfortable pause)* ... I'll talk to Thommassen about selling the shops.
NORA: Thank you, Johan. Uh ... have a nice stay in Copenhagen.
JOHAN: Thank you, Nora.
BOTH: *(They start talking at the same time)* It was nice seeing you again ... I'm so glad we had this time together ...

(They break off, laughing a little.)

JOHAN: Good luck, Nora, let me know what ...
NORA: Yes, I will ... Good-bye ...
JOHAN: Good-bye ...

(They shake hands, start off in opposite directions ... Music swells
    up ... They sing.)

(Music Cue 20H: I'm Making Love To You – Part III)

BOTH: *(Singing)*
BUT NO MATTER WHAT I SAY
OH, MY DEAR
CAN'T YOU HEAR?
I'M MAKING LOVE TO YOU!

(The lights fade to black.)

Scene Seven

(The Helmer living room.)
(NORA is alone, waiting.)
(TORVALD's voice can be heard off stage. NORA turns toward the door.)

TORVALD: *(Calling back to the children)* Children, go into the kitchen for your chocolate. Leave your sleds in the hallway!

(TORVALD enters, and is shocked to see NORA.)

NORA: Torvald ...
TORVALD: *(With ill-concealed anger)* How could you suddenly decide to visit us unannounced?
NORA: I need to talk to you.
TORVALD: *(Bitterly)* So you decided you can talk to a stranger?
NORA: When I left, it's true, you were a stranger, and I, too, was a stranger ... to myself. But I have learned through living who I am ...
TORVALD: I know you've become rich and successful and worldly.
NORA: I'm fit to share the children now, if you will only let me. I've so much more to give them ... I'm a woman, not a doll. May I see the children now?
TORVALD: Did you think you could come back here

expecting me conveniently to behave like some saint? Picture me Nora, the rejected husband – angry, humiliated, trying to hold my head up in this town among our friends and my colleagues. You left me and built a life of your own and I've had to build one too, here with the children. I can't let you see them.

NORA: My God, Torvald! Never to see my children!

TORVALD: The law is on my side.

NORA: Laws can be changed. People can change. I can't believe they're three rooms away from me and I can't ...

TORVALD: I said, "no"!

NORA: I'll fight you, Torvald. Some day, I'll win. Goodbye.

(She walks out the door ... the living room goes off or TORVALD exits. The action is continuous. We follow NORA without a break.)

(Outside, at a place nearby.)

(NORA is alone. The stage is bare. She breaks down sobbing and falls to the floor in a heap. Gradually, she pulls herself together and pulls herself back up to her feet. Absolutely alone in the world, she sings:)

(Music Cue 21: Finale)

WELL, LITTLE SPARROW, LITTLE SKYLARK,
WHAT NOW ... ?

(Music begins. She walks forward, gaining confidence as she does so, realizing that she can survive it all and go on.)

NORA, YOU'VE BEEN HERE BEFORE
SPREAD YOUR WINGS AND RISE ONCE MORE
YOU ARE YOUR ONE AND ONLY
LEARN TO LIVE
FLY ... NORA, FLY!

END OF PLAY